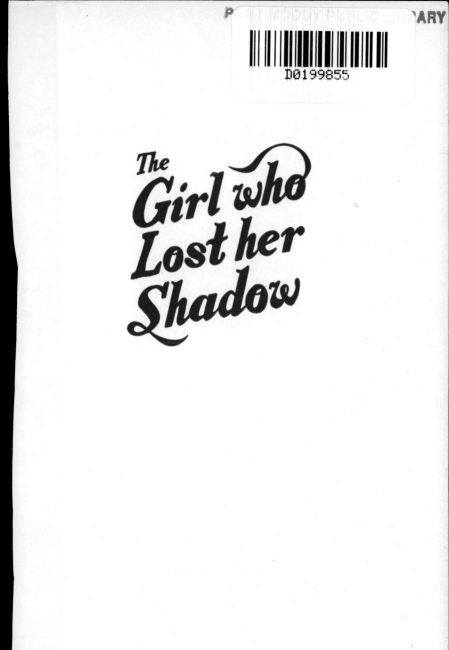

The
*Girl who
Lost her
Shadow*

Kelpies is an imprint of Floris Books
First published in 2019 by Floris Books
First published in North America in 2020
© 2019 Emily Ilett

The publisher acknowledges subsidy from Creative
Scotland towards the publication of this volume

 Also available as an eBook

British Library CIP data available
ISBN 978-178250-607-2
Typesetting by User Design, Illustration and Typesetting
Printed & bound by MBM Print SCS Ltd, Glasgow

 Floris Books supports sustainable forest management by
printing this book on materials made from wood that
comes from responsible sources and reclaimed material

MIX
Paper from
responsible sources
FSC® C117931

The Girl who Lost her Shadow

EMILY ILETT

Kelpies

Chapter One

Gail was eating cornflakes when her shadow disappeared. She didn't even really like cornflakes. It happened, she thought, between the third and fourth mouthful. She watched the shadow slip under the kitchen door, rippling like an eel into the garden, leaving Gail with an itch in her right foot and a dribble of milk on her chin. She wasn't surprised. Everything was falling apart, including her. And it was all Kay's fault.

Kay was Gail's sister. She was three years, four months and seven days older than Gail. She had two seaweed-green stripes in her twisty hair, a gold hoop in her nose and teeth so crooked they looked like they'd been caught mid-somersault. She'd been the best swimmer on the island ever since she first learned backstroke. But now she was sinking.

Gail pressed her face to the window and saw her shadow flicker through the grass. It was the morning of her twelfth birthday and it felt nothing like it should. Her dad had left two months ago, her mum was headed to work and Kay was in bed. Like she always was, now.

"Take this up to your sister, Gail honey." Her mum slid a plate of toast in front of her. "And don't eat all the cake."

Gail stared at the birthday cake. It looked like a cowpat. Brown icing dribbled in sticky globs onto the table. On the top, blue Smarties spelled out *Gale*. Spelling Gail 'Gale' was her dad's old, unfunny joke. He'd told her that on the night she was born, her screams were so fierce she'd drowned out the wail of the gale-force winds spinning around the hospital. That's why they'd named her Gail.

The fridge light blinked on and off as her mum rushed around the kitchen, checking that her sister's favourite dishes were still stocking every single shelf. It had been like this for weeks. Gail scowled. It was *her* birthday; Kay should be bringing *her* breakfast. Gail flicked her spoon and watched as a drop of milk sailed onto Kay's toast.

"Guess what, Mum? My shadow's disappeared."

"What's that, honey?" Her mum glanced towards the ceiling as the toilet flushed upstairs.

"It went right under the door. I saw it in the garden."

The wrinkles around her mum's dark eyes trembled as she forced a smile. "Is that right, honey? That sounds interesting. You'll tell me all about it later, won't you?" She rooted in her handbag for the keys. "Remember Kay's toast."

Gail scratched the itch on her right foot harder.

"She won't eat it."

Her mum was already marching towards the door, her nurse's uniform flapping like old pancakes behind her. "Kay loves Marmite," she said. At the door, she turned. "Hey, Gail." She paused. "Maybe Kay will want to swim today."

Gail glared after her. Kay hated Marmite and she never wanted to swim any more. They used to swim every week, but everything had changed after their dad left. Now, Kay never left her room if she could help it. She hardly ate, and if she looked at Gail, it was like she was looking all the way through her, as if she was invisible.

Today, invisible was exactly how Gail felt.

Gail stood up, picked a Smartie out of the 'a' in *Gale*, crunched down hard and pulled the plate of toast closer. The house felt too small for everything that was happening inside. It was like the air was being squeezed out of it, making it harder and harder to breathe.

With the toast in one hand, Gail climbed the stairs. Kay was in her bedroom staring out of the window onto the grey cracked wall of the newsagent next door. Gail could see that Kay's eyes were jellyfish-pink at the edges. She rubbed at them when Gail came in.

"Hey, happy birthday." Kay's voice was old and tired. "You're not in school?"

Gail balanced the plate on the bed. "It's Saturday." Kay never knew what day it was. She hadn't been to school since it started back after summer. She just slept all the time. The room stank of sleep. Kay's bedside lamp cast slippery shapes on the walls, which were covered with shiny posters of squid, sea-dragons and whales.

Gail took a deep breath. "I'm going down to the beach." She shrugged her shoulder towards the window. "Do you want to come? It's been ages since we swam."

Kay chewed her lower lip and Gail followed her gaze as her eyes shifted beyond the newsagent to the ocean, blue-grey and glittering beneath them.

It was Kay who'd first taught Gail to swim. Gail had swallowed chlorine in the town pool till she felt sick and dizzy, Kay's hands holding up her stomach. Then, when she'd learned breaststroke, they'd clambered down to the pebbly scrap of beach below their house, where the ocean sucked at the stones like sweets. Even in summer, the water was so cold it burned. Lifted by waves, they'd swap stories of deep-sea explorers, and imagine turtles and spider crabs beneath the surface whenever their toes brushed against something in the water. They'd dare each other to swim further and further and faster and faster, and do handstands underwater with their eyes open and stinging. They'd collect cowrie shells and razor clams, and one time Gail had found a dead starfish which they'd dissected later in the bath.

Each time they swam, waves rolled over them and through them like a whale's heartbeat, and they'd clutch each other's hands and lick salt from their lips and dream of diving in the reefs of Barbados and all the sea creatures they were going to care for or discover when they became marine biologists. Because they were always going to swim together. Always.

Gail tore her gaze from the heaving sea and stared at her sister. The green twist of Kay's hair hung limply against her face, and her eyes were flat and empty. It was as if a light inside her had gone out. "I want to go swimming, Kay. Come on, Mum says there's a big storm coming and we'll be stuck inside tomorrow."

Kay blinked and shook her head as if coming out of a deep sleep. "Hey," she said. "I forgot..." Reaching beneath the bed, she brought out a long tube. "Happy birthday, Sis."

Gail winced – Kay never called her *Sis* – and pulled the poster out of the tube. The glossy paper unfurled to reveal a giant manta ray, its fins sweeping like wings through the water. Gail stared at it. Manta rays were Kay's favourite sea creature. She must have bought the poster for herself a long time ago and forgotten about it. It wasn't meant for Gail at all.

"Do you like it?"

Gail swallowed and nodded. "Yeah. Thanks." Her hands tightened on the edges of the paper. "Are you coming swimming?"

Kay shook her head. "No. I don't think so."

Gail's fingers squeezed the poster harder. "Come on, you always say that. It's my birthday, Kay."

Kay turned away. "I don't want to."

"But it's my birthday!"

"I'm sorry, Gail. I can't. I... You go."

Blood rushed to Gail's cheeks. She couldn't go alone. They both wanted to be marine biologists but Gail was terrified of drowning. She never swam by herself. Kay knew that. A hot, prickly anger pulsed through Gail. "You don't want to do anything any more! All you do is sit here feeling sorry for yourself! Mum says you're ill but you're not really. You're just selfish!" Gail began tearing at the poster, ripping the manta ray into smaller and smaller pieces. "What about me, Kay?"

"Gail—" Kay began, her mouth open in shock.

"It's my birthday and I can't swim by myself and you just stay here staring with your stupid, selfish..."

"Don't..." Kay reached out to her but Gail wriggled away. Fragments of paper spilled onto Gail's feet and when she looked down her toes were covered in dark grey slices of manta ray.

"And my shadow's gone," she burst out, pressing her hands to her sides to stop them shaking. "You're meant to be the sick one, but yours is still here."

She kicked her foot against the carpet where Kay's light-grey shadow was poised, and a rush of something broken and hurting and heavy flooded her body, making her knees tremble. Gail staggered against the wall. Her feet prickled as Kay's shadow gathered around them, silken between her toes. She gasped at the force of it. She felt emptied of everything she cared about, hollow like a clam shell cast up on a beach. She tried to swallow the lump that was blocking her throat and making her eyes burn. Was this how Kay felt?

Then, before Gail's legs buckled completely, Kay's shadow silently slid away from her towards the door, as if it had somewhere else to be. At the edge of the carpet it paused, hesitating for a second, but then the dark shape tightened, as if a decision had been made, and the shadow slipped out of the room.

Kay's eyes widened as she stared at the empty places where their shadows should be. The floor looked embarrassed.

Gail held her breath.

"Get it back, Gail," Kay said at last. Her voice shivered and the hoop in her nose shone dimly. "Get it back."

Chapter Two

Rain tapped against the kitchen window as Gail stuffed sandwiches and gloves into her backpack. Next to the gloves she squeezed the red torch her mum had given her that morning, a birthday gift so Gail could watch the rock pools come alive with crabs after dark. Tucking her phone into the pocket of the bag, Gail pulled a face. She always took it with her, though there was never any signal on the island. Too many steep hills and valleys. On a corner of newspaper, its headlines warning of the next day's storm, she scrawled:

Gone to Rin's. Be back soon.

Rin was Gail's friend. Or she used to be.

How long would it take to find Kay's shadow? Gail's nose wrinkled. An hour? A day? She scowled at the downpour. Shadows were meant to stay stuck, like ears and promises. They weren't meant to run away.

They were especially not meant to run away when it was raining. Or on your birthday.

Gail's stomach twisted as she heard the bed creak upstairs. Kay's shadow hadn't just run away. It was Gail's fault. If she hadn't kicked it... The hurt in Kay's brown eyes bubbled in front of her. "I chased her shadow away," Gail said to the empty kitchen. She grabbed a photo of Kay from the fridge, stuffing it into her bag. "And now I'll get it back."

When she opened the door, the wind tugged at her hair. Gail squeezed her eyes against the rain, peering forward. Behind her house, the ground rose steeply towards Ben Fiadhaich, the wild hill. There it was: she could just make out the dark blur of Kay's shadow pouring over the damp grass at the end of their garden. Gail saw it flow over the wall towards the river, which tumbled icy-cold and fierce down the hillside. "Wait," she cried out, but the word was tugged from her lips by the wind and undone.

Rain soaked through her leggings as she ran down the garden and clambered over the wall. Here, a footpath curled along the river and out of the village for a mile, before forking into two: one beginning long-legged zigzags up the hillside, the other dipping to wind along the jagged cliff edge towards the south of the island. The shadow was metres in front of her, its shape shifting and swirling as it rolled over pebbles and through puddles.

Gail's legs burned as she tried to keep up, blinking rain out of her eyes. At least now she was out of the house she could breathe again. Her head didn't feel so squashed. And once she brought Kay's shadow home, maybe everything would go back to how it was before. Before their dad walked out. Before Kay got sick. Before she stopped swimming.

Gail swallowed.

It had to.

She was out of the village now. Ben Fiadhaich loomed on her left, its slope scattered with straggles of trees and ledges of rock where shallow caves pitted the hillside like eyes. Gail crossed her fingers, hoping that Kay's shadow would turn right towards the cliffs where kittiwakes wheeled and cried. But the dark shape slipped left at the fork, and Gail groaned and pressed her hands against her legs to push against the rise. No one climbed this side of Ben Fiadhaich. The slope was jagged and crumbling and there were too many whispered stories about the caves. *Lynx Cave, Oyster Cave, Cave of Thieves.*

The shadow slid in and out of her sight, slippery as a fish. It was moving further away. Now it left the path, darting over rocks and between tall pines.

Gail plunged through the grass, hands lurching to steady herself against the uneven ground. As she slalomed between trees, the rain petered to a fine drizzle. Here, the ground felt alive with shadows, stretching and reaching towards her. Which one was Kay's? How would she know? But as she saw a dark shape sweeping over the grass, her mouth twitched in relief. Of course she'd know Kay's shadow. It was like recognising her sister's handwriting, or hearing the sound of her footsteps on the stairs.

Gail fought to make her legs move faster but the shadow was always ahead of her. Her chest heaving in waves, she tried to sprint but a stitch pierced her side and she folded over, clutching her stomach. "I can't," she gasped, and she crumpled to the ground. And she lay, panting for breath, her legs stuck out in front of her, as the shadow moved steadily up the hillside, closer and closer to the caves.

Gail had short legs, big feet and seal-dark eyes that were fond of staring. Her brown cheeks were dotted with so many freckles it looked like a bowl of Coco Pops had been tipped onto them. Beneath her coat and jumper, she wore a tawny-orange T-shirt which almost reached her knees, and her sodden leggings were zigzagged blue and green. When she talked, her whole face moved, and when she ran she jumped high in the air so as not to trip over her feet. But she tried not to run if she could help it. She was a swimmer, not a runner. Gail winced. And not much of a swimmer either, without Kay.

Gail was higher and further from the village than she'd thought. Below, the island rolled down from Ben Fiadhaich, speckled with villages and towns and silver beaches. She could see the harbour to her right, reaching out towards the mainland, where her mum worked at the hospital. Fishing boats and ferries dotted the sea. Fiorport, the harbour town, was where Gail went to her new high school. She'd been looking forward to starting for months, looking forward to Kay showing her around. But then Kay hadn't started back after summer and Gail caught the bus alone each morning, her mouth a thin silent line. Her friends had tried to understand, for a bit. But now they'd given up. Even Rin had stopped sitting next to her at lunch.

"You don't seem like *you* any more," she'd said. "You've changed, Gail."

Gail grimaced. She had changed. Just like Kay had. It began when they stopped swimming together. Her edges felt wobbly and uncertain. No wonder her shadow had run away.

As a bubble of anger grew inside her, the stitch in Gail's side prickled and she pushed her hands against it, below her ribs. It felt like a pufferfish. The spikes made her fists tighten and a flood of scarlet blotched her throat and ears. Gail took a deep breath. It had been two weeks after their dad left that she'd first felt the pufferfish inside her stomach.

On that evening, when the light had already begun to seep from her sister's eyes, she'd found a crab shell speckled like a starry night sky and had taken it to show Kay. It was beautiful, covered in hundreds of tiny galaxies, and inside it was the purple of blackberry stains and twilight. Kay wouldn't even look at it, her back curved against Gail, eyes half-closed. So Gail had pressed it into Kay's hand, but she'd pressed too hard and the shell had crumbled like dust between their fingers. Kay had turned around then, flicking at the broken pieces of shell on her duvet, her eyes cold. She'd said that *real* marine biologists didn't break stuff.

It was then that Gail had first felt a sharp blossom of spikes in her stomach and a flare of anger that made her crush the last of the starry shell in her own fist. Since then, the pufferfish inside her stomach kept her awake at night. Anger bubbled through her all the time and she couldn't make it stop.

Gail took a deep gulp of air. Kay would make it stop. Once Gail got her shadow back, everything would return to normal.

From where she sat, halfway up Ben Fiadhaich, Gail could just make out the dip of the beach where she'd found the crab shell. There, the rock pools swam with anemones, sea urchins and snails. She could see the path that they'd fly down most days, all the way to the water. Before school, after school, weekends. Birthdays.

Some mornings the ocean was almost too blue to believe in. Other days, they darted from the grey rush of it, daring each other to stand further and further out on the rocks so that they came home soaked and shivering, the dare shining out of their eyes. Kay always went further than Gail. Always two steps closer to the edge.

The drizzle had stopped. Gail bit her lip and lurched to her feet, turning away from her home towards the south of the island. Here, the ground rose knuckled and gnarled. Around the dark tangle of Grimloch Woods, hills towered, threatening as shark fins, their sides tumbling down into steep valleys and lochs where the cold, luminous water seemed to reflect skies from whole other worlds. It was a long and treacherous hike to reach the sharp southern tip of the island, where the ocean lashed at the cliffs and the path crumbled into jagged arches. Few people walked that way, and even fewer lived there.

Gail and Kay had often talked about that journey to the southern tip. They knew that was where the Storm Sisters were, two huge rocks standing right on the edge of the cliff. The story went that the Storm Sisters were giants turned to stone many years ago. People said that the Sisters protected the island, calling the ocean to batter hardest against their faces and spare the rest of the coast. As soon as they'd heard the story, Kay was enthralled. She suggested they hike south and look for them and they'd spent hours planning what they'd take and when they'd go.

But that was before everything had changed.

Gail turned back to the hillside, scanning the slopes for her sister's shadow. Where had it gone? She hurried upwards, her eyes darting from side to side until – wait, was that it? Gail straightened, her hand shielding her eyes. There it was. A dark blur, paused near—

Her stomach flipped.

The shadow hovered at the entrance to Oyster Cave.

For a wild moment, Gail thought it was waiting for her. But then it shuddered, the darkness within it trembling, and Gail remembered that she was the one who had chased it away. "No," she called out, as the shadow slid towards the gaping hole. "Wait!"

she shouted, and her eyes widened as she saw the shadow steady for a moment, then twitch and slip neatly into the cave opening.

Chapter Three

The cave arched open like an oyster shell, wrinkled and gnarled at the edges and narrowing towards a closed hinge at the back. At the far end, where the rock closed together, a small low opening continued into the darkness. Big enough for a child to crawl through; too small for an adult. Kay's shadow was nowhere to be seen.

The cave's name rippled through homes across the island. Oyster Cave. Everyone knew someone who knew a story about it. *Oyster Cave's where the selkies leave their skins, you can smell the damp fur when the wind's blowing in the right direction. Did you hear about the boy that went missing in the cave? They found him weeks later, nesting with the birds...*

And, Kay's voice, last summer: "They didn't speak for days afterwards. They couldn't. Every time they opened their mouths, nothing came out."

She'd whispered it with something like awe mixed

in with her mouthful of spaghetti. Two girls and a boy from her class had spent the night in the cave, had crawled through to the network of tunnels beyond. The next day, they'd stumbled into the village, dull-eyed and silent.

"Why couldn't they speak?" Gail had asked as her sister's nose wrinkled in delight at the story.

"They were lost in there for hours, Gail. Hours and hours in the darkness, trying to get out. Imagine it." Kay's voice dropped. "Maybe they *saw* something..."

Their mum grunted, spooning more spaghetti onto their plates. "More likely they frightened themselves stupid with ghost stories," she said. "But no one knows how far those tunnels go, so don't either of you be going anywhere near them."

Kay grinned and Gail saw her fingers crossed beneath the table when she nodded. Later, skin prickling with stories, Gail had made Kay promise not to go without her.

But now she had to leave Kay behind.

Gail pulled the torch out of her bag and stepped inside the cave. Salt stung her nostrils. Her feet felt colder without her shadow and she stamped on the ground to warm them.

Of course Kay's shadow would be the most awkward

shadow ever. Why would a shadow run away to the deepest, darkest, stinkiest place it could think of? Gail grimaced and shoved her backpack through the hole ahead of her. Falling to her stomach, she wriggled through the gap at the back of the cave, pieces of grit showering her shoulders.

The tunnel soon opened up and after a metre or so she could stand again. The air was furry, like spider's legs, and Gail felt the darkness in her mouth like it was a solid thing. Her hands trembled as she switched on her new torch and the tunnel became alive with lumpy columns of rock and knots of shadows.

Gail shrank back against the damp wall. She moved the torch slowly, shadows twitching and flitting around the light like shoals of sardines.

"Kay? Kay's shadow?" Her voice was thin and the rock echoed it back to her, broken and confused.

K

    A y   s   d

O   w

        h   s

      a

Gail inched forwards, the torchlight catching the curve of the tunnel. She rounded the corner and yelped, her breath puffing out in a white cloud of shock as she stumbled backwards.

There, swimming through the cave wall, was a manta ray.

It was huge and beautiful, almost as wide as Gail's outstretched arms, its mouth reaching up to the tunnel roof. Its dark fins stretched out like wings, with flashes of white at their tips, and its tail flicked to the left. Gail's heart pounded at the familiarity of the shape. This was Kay's ray. A giant oceanic manta ray with a white underside. She drew it everywhere, always this same shape, until she said it was as easy as writing her own name. How was it here?

She inched closer to the drawing. Was it ancient? Gail reached a hand to it, breathing softly. Her fingertips grazed the surface and whitened. Chalk. Gail spat on her fingers, rubbed at more of the drawing, and the ray's edge blurred and disappeared beneath her hand.

"But this is new. This is—" Gail spun around, her back tensed against the presence of someone else in the tunnels.

She only saw slips of shadows disappear beyond the torch beam, and the cloud of her own breath in the air.

She remembered when Kay had drawn chalk outlines of lion's mane jellyfish on the tarmac outside their house. They'd glowed there for a week until the rain had washed them off. Here, the cave walls were damp and streaked with lichen. Someone must have drawn it in the last few days. But who would draw something here? And who would draw Kay's ray? Surely... For a moment, Gail wavered. "No," she said aloud, shaking the thought away. "She couldn't have." Kay hadn't left the house for a long while.

The drawing made Gail's skin tingle, as if something floated past her in the darkness, brushing against her arm. As she turned away, the torch flickered over a smudge in the eye of the ray. Gail hesitated. There was a small hole in the rock face, just a few inches above her head. The ray had been carefully drawn around it. The tingling in Gail's skin grew as she reached up to the small shelf.

When her fingers touched something rough and sharp-edged, Gail flinched then pulled it out of the hole. Her eyes widened at what she'd found. A shell, larger than her hand. The underside was a dark burgundy brown with fine ridges like the bark of a tree, and when she turned it over, the inner glowed gently, milky pale with yellow spots. It was a mussel shell, the biggest one she'd seen.

Gail stroked the inside with her thumb and frowned as she felt something crinkle beneath her fingertips. She tipped the shell away from her and the light revealed a thin layer of tissue paper, folded over and over, slipped inside. Gail pulled it out carefully, opening the sheet until it lay flat across her hand. She realised she was holding her breath and let it out slowly, excitement bubbling in her chest. It was a map. A map inside a shell.

Shifting her palm so the light could catch the whisker-thin lines, she tried to make sense of what she saw: a series of small drawings sketched across a sharp-pointed finger of land. One drawing was of a pine tree, its middle branch sticking out with a spray of firs on its tip like a hand; next to it was a moon-shaped loch in a low valley. Gail chewed her lip, questions fizzing in her mind. Where was this? And who was it for?

She stared accusingly at the map, demanding it be less cryptic. Then she looked back at the manta ray. Her finger traced the shape of it in the air, just as she'd seen Kay draw it, over and over again, everywhere she could. Gail blinked. Of course. Someone else knew about Kay's manta. And they must have drawn this one for her, so she'd stop and find the shell. The map was waiting for Kay, like a secret.

A flood of jealousy washed through Gail. Kay had never had secrets from her before.

She turned the map over slowly in her hands. Whoever left this for Kay couldn't know that her sister was sinking. That she didn't leave the house, didn't pick up her phone. Whoever left this for Kay didn't know she wouldn't find it. And it must be important. No one entered Oyster Cave unless they had to.

Something whispered like a trapped breeze further down the tunnel and Gail's eyes widened guiltily. She'd forgotten Kay's shadow. She had to catch up with it; the map would have to wait. Shoving the shell and paper into her pocket, she broke into a run, her torch beam ricocheting off the walls. The tunnel narrowed so that Gail's elbows jarred on the rock and she sucked in her cheeks with the pain. The tang of salt creased her nose as the ground began to slope downwards. She'd been running in a steady curve to the right, so she must be close to the ocean now. The air was green with the smell of seaweed.

Suddenly, the tunnel split into two. Gail pushed her fringe out her eyes and gasped for breath. Which way? She pointed the torchlight as far as she could down each side of the split but could see nothing. Her skin prickled.

"Kay's shadow," she whispered. Nothing happened.

She said it again, louder: "Kay's shadow?"

This time the rocks picked at her words, shaking them around and around like a handful of grit, until they fell apart.

S   ha d   o w
      ow   d
              a   s h
      h   ad   so
  w
              d o w   ash
h o w   s a d

How sad shadow, the cave echoed, and Gail's stomach twisted inside her. She squeezed her eyes shut and marched forward, taking whichever tunnel her feet took her into.

"It's not sad," she muttered, her hands reaching out in the darkness around her. "It's not fair. I'm lost and—aieeggh—" Gail's eyes snapped open as her elbow jarred with something soft, but her scream was cut off by a small cold hand pressed firmly over her mouth. A hand belonging to whatever she'd just walked into, in the darkness of Oyster Cave, where anyone could disappear.

Chapter Four

Blinking furiously, Gail tried to breathe through her nose. Her hand pressed against the damp rock of the tunnel wall to steady herself, but still, everything trembled. Her knees shook and something watery was happening to her eyes. At least the hand looked human, she thought.

Gail tilted her head, running her eyes back from the hand up the pale arm to an orange fizz of hair. The hair was smiling at her. That wasn't right. Gail closed her eyes. When she opened them again, the smile grew broader and the hair twitched away to reveal a girl. When Gail met her eyes, the girl grinned, put her finger to her lips and took her hand away from Gail's mouth.

Gail took a deep breath and lifted her own hand to scrub her mouth, but the girl grabbed it mid-journey and began shaking it with delight.

"Is mise Mhirran," she whispered, walking Gail

hastily back the way she'd come. "Dè an t-ainm a th'ort?" Gail stared blankly at the Gaelic she'd never learned and the girl's grin widened as she began a strange thumb-and-elbow dance with Gail's arm. "I'm Mhirran." She jerked her shoulder backwards. "Sorry about that. I didn't want my brother to know I'd sneaked off." Mhirran's eyes glittered with excitement. "You're the second person I've ever met in these tunnels." She looked around them. "I don't know why no one else comes down here, aren't they just beautiful?"

Gail looked doubtfully around her.

"I came in through the Cave of Thieves." Mhirran was still talking. "How about you? Ooo, did you hear my Morse code? Is that why you've come? It went like this. *Taptaptaptap tap tapscrapetaptap tapscrapetaptap scrapescrapescrape*. It's how I talk to the stalactites. Listen."

Gail stared in confusion at the girl tapping earnestly on the rock. She was Gail's height but it looked like she should have been taller. Her shoulders were stooped as if they were having a conversation with her knees. Her teeth flashed silvery with braces and she had more freckles even than Gail. Her hair was clementine orange and seemed constantly surprised, and her glasses slid off her nose as she talked, even though her nose was the kind of nose that should really keep glasses up. Gail realised she'd seen Mhirran near the village a couple of times before. She was younger than Gail, ten probably. But she'd never seen her in school.

"I guess you didn't hear it," Mhirran said, turning around.

Gail shook her head. "I don't think so," she said at last, a twinge of apology in her voice.

Mhirran pushed her glasses up her nose. "Maybe I'm just not loud enough." She sighed, then immediately brightened. "Which way did you come? Did you come from Oyster Cave or from the sea?" She jerked her thumb backwards towards the fork where the salt had stung Gail's nostrils. "There's a drawing near Oyster Cave. Did you see it? He's so good at them. Is the tide out or did you swim in? I bet you swam, you look like a swimmer. Did you?"

Gail winced but Mhirran didn't wait for an answer.

"I've seen dolphins near Seal Cave. They came so close I was scared they were lost. I wish I could have dunked my face in the water to talk with them." Mhirran paused, threw her head back and gave a series of bizarre clicks and whistles ending with a prolonged squeak. "What do you think?"

Despite herself, Gail laughed. Mhirran's impression was uncannily good. "You speak Dolphin?"

The girl beamed. "I could teach you. I speak all sorts of—"

"MHIRRAN!" A sharp voice echoed through the tunnels behind them.

Mhirran rolled her eyes then grinned at Gail. "I have to go, but see you around! You should head this way," she said, as she pointed to the other tunnel in the fork. "That'll take you out." And then she was gone.

Silence settled around Gail. The dark seemed darker and Gail felt suddenly very alone. Little by little, the rush of Mhirran's words washed through her. Morse code. Talking with dolphins. The Sea Cave where you can swim inside the tunnels. The drawing at Oyster Cave. Gail's hand went to her pocket and she pulled out the shell. So Mhirran had seen the drawing too. Gail chewed her lip and froze. Wait, what had she said? *He's so good at them.*

Gail started forward. Mhirran knew who'd done the manta ray. Was it her brother? Hurrying after her, Gail heard a muffled exclamation ahead. A clatter and shout echoed down the tunnel. She hesitated, uncertainty slowing her feet. Why had Mhirran told Gail to go the other way?

Gail pressed her lips together. She wanted to know who'd done the drawing. She'd just have a look. She'd stay hidden.

Switching off her torch, she inched forward with one hand on the wall. To her surprise, the tunnel wasn't completely dark: dusty light hung in curtains ahead of her. Gail stopped before a sharp bend. She could make out words now.

"You didn't listen. I told you to let go of the rope when you saw one." The boy's voice was lemony-sour. Like all the life had been squeezed out of it. Gail pressed her body against the rock.

"But I did let go," came Mhirran's reply. She sounded strangely subdued.

"You let go too late. You just stood and watched it go by. It went right past you!"

"I didn't see it."

"You weren't paying attention."

Silence vibrated through the tunnel. Gail frowned. Apart from it wasn't silent at all. If she held her breath, she could hear a quiet low whirring, like a motor.

"I don't even know why I let you come." There was the sound of something scraping along the ground. "Keep your eyes open next time."

"My eyes *were* open. They were just looking in the wrong place." Mhirran hesitated, then her voice brightened. "Did you know that mantis shrimp can move their eyes in different directions?"

Gail's mouth bent into a lopsided smile. She knew that.

"I guess if I had eyes at the end of my arms, that'd be easier. Then I wouldn't have missed it."

An angry snort from the boy.

"Like starfish. Which don't even have brains," Mhirran continued.

Gail giggled before she could cover her mouth and the voices immediately stopped.

Footsteps snapped over the stone towards her.

"Who's there?"

Unsure whether to run or reveal herself, Gail spun around, but as she did so, she caught her foot on a rock, lost her balance and stumbled forward, tripping onto something hard and wooden which cracked sickeningly beneath her.

When she opened her eyes, her nose was inches away from a dark splinter of wood which pointed at her accusingly amongst a ruin of planks and nails. Gail tasted blood where she'd bitten her cheek as she fell, and her ribs throbbed. Untangling her ankles from her knees, she glanced upwards.

"Move." The word slid like a sea snake towards her.

Gail flinched. A boy, around Kay's age, crouched over her. His dark hair was cut short above his face, which was made entirely of angles. His nose was pointed and sharp as a goblin shark and he was holding a slice of wood in his hand, the jagged edge an inch away from Gail's chest.

Gail struggled backwards, kicking away pieces of rope. "I'm sorry, I—"

The boy's eyes glittered. Gail was pressed against the cave wall. Sweat dribbled over her lip.

"You're sorry? That's it? Do you—"

He paused, his head turned to one side. Behind him, Gail could see beyond the bend in the tunnel where she'd been listening. She peered into a large cavern, squinting against the thin light which dripped in through a crescent-shaped hole in the roof. Around her, stalactites and stalagmites chewed through the cavern like teeth. Something clanked and popped; the slow whirring that Gail had heard before was sputtering to a stop. The sound was coming from the far side of the cavern where a large wooden chest with a gaping canvas funnel strapped tightly to one side vibrated in gurgles and burps. It looked like a bigger version of what was now scattered in pieces around Gail. Next to the chest was Mhirran. Her cheeks were flushed and her eyes looked everywhere but the boy's face.

"I didn't do anything," Mhirran said. "It just...?"

The boy's thin lips tightened as he threw down

the wooden splinter, striding towards the chest, and pushing Mhirran out of the way.

Steadying herself on a stalactite, Mhirran caught Gail's eye and tried to wink but failed. She walked over and offered a hand to help Gail up.

"That's your brother?" Gail whispered to her, making a face.

Mhirran's gaze shifted to where the boy crouched next to the machine. An expression Gail didn't understand flitted across her face, then was gone. She shrugged. "I told you to go the other way."

Gail stepped closer to Mhirran, her voice low and urgent. "But I had to ask you something. You said you saw the manta ray, the drawing, near Oyster Ca..." Her words trickled away as she felt the prickle of the boy watching her from where he crouched by the chest. He wasn't looking at her face. His eyes were fixed on her feet and his mouth twitched as if something pulled at it. He picked up her torch from where it had rolled and flickered the beam across the cave floor towards her. Before it reached her feet, Gail stepped back behind a stalagmite thicker than her waist.

Mhirran peered at her around the stalagmite, her hand curled around the gnarls and rings of its growth.

"Are you looking for Femi?" she asked.

Gail frowned. "Who? No. I'm looking for—"

She broke off. Something cold hovered at her side.

"She's looking for her shadow. Aren't you?" The torch beam swung pointedly at her feet where her shadow should have been. The boy leaned over her.

Gail swallowed.

"I'm sorry about our... misunderstanding." He waved his hand towards where Gail had fallen, his eyes still hard. "Let's start again. I'm Francis," he said. "And you are?"

For a minute, Gail thought furiously of other names she could be called. She didn't want this goblin shark knowing her name. But her mind remained unhelpfully blank. "Gail," she muttered.

"Gail," Francis repeated, with a smirk. "A strange name for a girl without a shadow."

Gail turned to Mhirran, who was looking at the place where Gail's shadow wasn't with a mixture of horror and pity. Her eyes were huge with it.

"What's wrong with my name?" Gail demanded, but Francis just raised his eyebrows, his smile sharp with teeth. "And I'm not looking for my shadow," she said. "You don't know anything about me!"

Francis's reply slunk across the space between them.

"Do *you*?" he asked.

Chapter Five

Gail thought up mean insults about Francis's nose, turned her back on him and kicked her shoe against the ground, wincing when she bruised a toe. Of course she knew who she was. She was Gail. She had big feet, a scar on her knee, too many freckles, and lived with her mum and sister on a stormy Scottish island far away from where all the really cool fish were. The ones with the warts and the colours and the weird mouths.

Gail grimaced. She had no friends, no shadow, cold feet, and she was very lost in a cave deep inside Ben Fiadhaich. She was scared of things she'd never been scared of before and she hadn't swum for weeks. Since Kay had started sinking, Gail had changed too. *Did* she know who she was any more?

Gail scrunched up her face and stormed towards the tunnels at the far side of the cavern, her hands on her hips.

Mhirran hurried after her.

"Wait, where are you going?" she whispered. "Gail, I can he—"

"Do you know how many tunnels lead off these three, Gail?" Francis called out behind her, his voice cold and precise. "Seventeen. Seventeen tunnels. One goes back into the hill for miles, another curls around itself into a spiral, getting tighter and tighter and tighter, until it suddenly stops. And then there's the one that doesn't end. No one has got far enough in to know how long it is."

Gail shivered, the hairs on her arms crackling. "I'll find my way," she retorted.

"I knew someone who got lost in here for a month." Francis paused. "She must have been about your age."

Gail spun around to face him. Francis's hands twitched as his gaze fell towards her feet and lingered. Gail started at the glint of greed in his eye.

"But that won't happen to you, Gail, will it? Because you found us." Francis bent to pick a piece of rope off the ground, tightening it around his wrist over and over. "Lucky for you, really."

Gail screwed up her face but her heart sank. *Seventeen tunnels?* She didn't have enough food. She'd starve if she got lost. She couldn't get lost – she had to find Kay's shadow.

"I think you should come with us, Gail." Francis's

voice drew closer, each syllable sharp as the spine of a lionfish. "We've almost finished collecting for the day." He smiled.

Gail shivered. *Collecting?* Turning to Mhirran, she whispered under her breath. "I'm looking for my sister's shadow, Mhirran, not mine. It was right ahead of me in the tunnel. Did you see it?"

Mhirran's face paled. Her freckles stood out against her skin and she lifted her finger to her lips involuntarily before gesturing to Francis. He was staring at them both – Gail to Mhirran and back to Gail, his finger tapping a slow, slow rhythm on the wooden chest.

"Mhirran," Francis said at last, his eyes unreadable in the dim light. "Why don't you go ahead down the far tunnel and check everything is in order. It seems a shame not to finish what we started. And check them properly this time; someone's been tampering with them. Gail and I will take this tunnel to our uncle's and we'll meet you there. Gail doesn't want to wait around for us, do you, Gail? It'll give us a chance to learn more about each other. And your missing shadow," he added, an edge to his voice.

His lips hovered into what Gail supposed was meant to be a smile. It made her own mouth wince.

This plan was all wrong. Gail could feel the wrongness of it wash through her.

Orange hair itched against her cheek as Mhirran moved to stand beside her. The young girl's fingers wound around each other as she lifted her chin to face her brother.

"Gail will come with me. This way's the quickest way out and we're hungry." Mhirran smiled nervously. "And you've still got work to do here. I'll check the tunnel, like you said, and we'll meet you at home."

Francis half-stepped forward, his mouth a thin tightrope.

"And you'll move quicker, by yourself," Mhirran murmured softly. "You're bound to catch up with it that way."

Gail frowned. Catch up with what? Her head swam with questions.

But Mhirran was already pulling her to the far passage, leading her away from Francis, and her voice dropped to a whisper. "If you get lost, you'll never find the shadow, Gail. It's true what he said about the tunnels. And I can help you."

Gail hesitated.

"And you wanted to know about the drawing?" Mhirran added, her grip tightening on Gail's arm, pulling her away from the cavern.

Thick wet darkness enveloped them. Mhirran had taken Gail's torch from Francis's hand. Now she passed it to Gail, turning on her own as she jogged in an awkward hop-lurch-stride along the tunnel. Once they'd left the cavern behind them, the relief of getting away from Francis swept through Gail. She loosened, wobbling her arms like tentacles.

Gail didn't understand Francis and Mhirran's cryptic conversation. She didn't know what the strange funnel machine was, or what the siblings were doing in the caves, but she was glad of Mhirran's company. This tunnel was not like the last. The air tasted sour. It stuck between her teeth like strings of old nectarine. The walls were pitted with alcoves, and when sudden forks appeared, Mhirran steered them left or right without stopping to think. Her hair shone in the gloom like a flame, and Gail clung onto it with the hope that she was following the path of Kay's shadow. It couldn't have gone too far ahead. And Mhirran had said she would help.

Beside her, Mhirran chattered as if there was nothing to explain at all. Her voice darted from one thing to another.

"I never get lost down here." Mhirran patted the

rock affectionately, as she led them to the left of a wide fork. "I always find my way out. I'm like a limpet, you know, they always find their way home, back to their bit of the rock. This one needs a bit of help, though." Mhirran pointed to her toe and Gail discovered that what she'd thought was a clump of mud stuck to the girl's boot was, in fact, a small limpet, holding on tightly to her blue wellington. "I discovered it there this morning. I don't know how it got there, or why it chose my boot. I guess it got lost. But I think I know where it came from so I'm going to take it back." She reached down and patted the top of its shell thoughtfully. "Leo, I've called it. Leo the Limpet. The homes the limpets make on the rocks are called home scars. Do you have any scars? I got one on my shoulder when I was talking to a kittiwake one morning and walked straight into a hawthorn."

Without catching her breath or waiting for Gail to reply, Mhirran whistled a low note which echoed along the rock, dipping and diving through the darkness.

"Did you know that some languages have whistling sounds and people can talk through their whistles even when they're miles and miles and miles apart? Imagine that. We could whistle to my uncle to make us a sandwich already..." Mhirran whistled again, an odd tune that sounded as if it had sprained an ankle.

She grinned at Gail. "My uncle taught me. And lots of other things. I can do semaphore too. Watch."

Mhirran raised her left arm so it was straight out from her side, and her right arm hovered lower, sticking out at an angle. "See this is an M. M for... Marmite, Mouse, Manatee..."

"Manta ray," Gail said quietly and her heart squeezed against her ribs. "Mhirran. Back in the cavern, before I fell inside, did you see a shadow? My sister's shadow? It must have gone right by you."

Mhirran stumbled and Gail grabbed her arm to steady her. She coughed as dirt cascaded from the wall Mhirran had fallen into. "Bleurgh. Thanks." Mhirran rubbed her nose, pushed up her glasses and peered forward. When she spoke next, her voice was watery, like there was too much movement behind the words. "All the paths on this side of the cavern lead out to Grimloch Woods. We'll be there soon, this tunnel is only a mile long..."

Impatience rose in Gail's throat. "But did you see it, Mhirran? You must have. I have to know. I have to get it back." Gail's torchlight caught the corner of a small wooden chest at the side of the tunnel. Her stomach turned as she stepped closer. "What's this? It looks like a... trap. What is your brother doing? He's not like you. He's—"

As the torchlight caught the edge of Mhirran's face, Gail wished she could bite back her words. Mhirran's eyes were pressed shut behind her glasses and her mouth trembled like something caught in a net. Gail had forgotten how young she was.

"He told you," Mhirran muttered at last. "He's a collector. That's normal. People collect lots of different things. Stamps. Rocks." Her voice slowly brightened. "Shells. Starfish. Watch where you're walking; I need to check this chest and two more further up. It won't take long but I'll run ahead." She grinned. "Whistle if you need me."

Gail stared as Mhirran hurried forward, clutching the torch. *That wasn't an answer, Mhirran. And who collects starfish?*

As Mhirran passed the contraption on the floor, Gail noticed that she stumbled a little and her left foot crunched onto something hard.

"Whoops," Mhirran murmured.

Gail glanced over her shoulder. If Francis had seen that... No wonder he was annoyed at his sister, Gail thought. Mhirran was the clumsiest girl she'd ever met.

As she followed behind, Gail strained to see what Mhirran was doing. The second chest also looked like a miniature version of the one in the cavern. It had a funnel made of thick canvas attached to one end, like it was going to suck something inside it. *Like a vampire squid*, Gail thought. As Mhirran kneeled by the chest, Gail was sure she saw a dark flicker move across the funnel, flitting out over the stone. She stood chewing her lip as Mhirran disappeared around a curve in the rock. What would anyone go underground to collect?

Far ahead of her, Gail could hear the steady stream of Mhirran's chatter. "Can you hear the bats? They make me think of slippers but I don't know why..."

"Mhirran," she called. "Wait up." But Mhirran didn't hear her.

Gail groaned, readying to run after her. But she couldn't. Something had happened to her feet. They felt huge and heavy at the end of her legs, as if they were stuck to the ground. Gail gritted her teeth and grabbed at the wall, trying to pull herself forward, but it felt like she was swimming against a deep-sea current. And the current was getting stronger.

Gail looked down in horror at her shoes.

"Move," she ordered. She tried to tug her feet from the floor but they wouldn't budge. She tried to squeeze her fingers between her shoe and the rock but they wouldn't fit. "Move," she said again, her voice rising in her throat. "*Move*."

There was nothing beneath her feet but a shadow.

Gail swallowed hard. The shadow wasn't hers. It was longer than Gail, and fatter, though from her shoes it narrowed lumpily into a flat tip. Darkness pulsed within it. The shadow stuck to Gail's feet and held on tightly. It was a stalagmite's shadow. She could feel the rockiness of it spreading through her toes; they felt crumbly and solemn. Her shins began to harden and her kneecaps felt volcanic.

"Get off me!" Gail wrenched at her legs. She thought she heard an answering cry ahead of her. A little way behind, a scattering of grit fell to the ground and Gail froze. Francis's too-sharp face bloomed in her mind, and sweat dripped from her nose.

"I am not a rock," she stammered. "I'm just Gail. Just stupid, cold, wet, lost Gail. I am not a rock." Her hands shook as she strained against the shadow.

The tunnel puzzled out her name, shaking it around like a toy.

A L I G, it repeated.

Gail gritted her teeth. "It's Gail," she repeated. "Gail."

L I A G, the cave echoed.

There was a spatter of grit behind her.

Gail bit down hard on her lip. What should she do? What would Kay do? Then she knew.

"ILAG," she shouted. "GILA. GIAL. LAIG."

And, in return, the tunnel whispered, *G...A...I...L.*

With the gigantic relief that comes from someone recognising who you are, Gail broke free of the rock shadow and hurtled on towards Mhirran.

Chapter Six

Gail's nose arrived in Mhirran's armpit at the same time her knee arrived in her shoe and both of them collapsed in a heap on the ground. Gail spat out a soggy mulch of jumper.

"I think you've broken my armpit," Mhirran said, rubbing at it mournfully.

Gail's breath beat like waves in her throat. "I got stuck inside a shadow," she gasped, her eyes wide and gleaming.

Mhirran blinked. "What?"

"I couldn't move my feet, they were stuck. And I felt all..." The memory pulled Gail's face into a wince. She shivered it away. "It felt all wrong."

Mhirran was oddly silent, chewing at her lip.

"Like it was glue or a swamp or something, or like a magnet. But it was just a shadow." Gail leaned back against the side of the tunnel, her eyes chasing shadows on the ground around her. Everywhere darkness shifted and danced, swaying in the torchlight like seaweed underwater. Gail squeezed her eyes shut and turned her cheek against the cold rock. Her hands curled around the bottom of her feet protectively. "It got inside me, Mhirran. The shadow got inside me and I could feel what it was. I was becoming a rock." Gail shuddered. Nausea rolled around her stomach and she spat on the ground beside her.

When Gail finally opened her eyes, Mhirran was staring hard at a spider that was investigating her knee. "You know spiders can communicate through their webs, like playing guitar strings."

"Mhirran, listen! A rock shadow stuck to my feet! You said you know these tunnels, has that ever happened before?"

Mhirran's glasses slipped down her nose and when she pushed them up, she left a long trail of dirt down her face. Her eyes flickered between Gail's elbow and her chin. "Well, I don't know... I've heard some things."

"Like what?"

"Like, if you lose your shadow, other shadows – shadows that have got lost or confused or have run away – they can, kind of, grab onto you, because..." Mhirran's voice trailed away. She rubbed her nose. "I don't remember why," she muttered.

Gail fell back against the rock. How could she find Kay's shadow when she could be grabbed by other shadows at any moment? She watched the spider scuttle from Mhirran's hand across the ground. Could she get caught by an insect's shadow? Or a bat's? For a second, Gail allowed herself to miss her own shadow. Her stomach twisted and a lump grew in her throat. She was sure Mhirran knew more than she was telling. The space between them felt soupy with secrets.

Gail's hand traced a faint bump on the side of her ankle where a thin scar was hidden behind her sock. She'd got it one late afternoon when she'd been with Kay, both of them hopping around the beach to warm up after a swim. Gail had twisted her foot on the sharp ridges of a shell and sliced open the skin of her ankle. Blood dribbled from the wound and Gail had avoided Kay's eyes, pretending it was nothing, while she bit back tears. Kay would make her wash it in the sea; the cut was already gritty with sand. But to Gail's surprise, Kay had picked up the shell and spun it around to look inside the hole.

"I'll bet a hermit crab once lived in this," she'd said. "You know they pass on shells when they get too big for them. All the hermit crabs on the beach line up biggest to smallest and pass the shells down the line."

Gail's cheeks were sodden with tears, but Kay had

ignored them, staring at her seriously and placing the shell carefully on her head. "I reckon this one fits you, Mistress Hermit," she'd said.

Despite herself, Gail had giggled, straightening to keep the shell balanced.

Kay had found her own shell, balanced it on her head and made her hands into pincers. They flapped around Gail's face, prodding and pinching at her nose and cheeks until she'd felt her hands become pincers too. The sisters stumbled around the beach, pinching each other's noses, trying to grab each other's shells, until, with a cry that stung everything out of her, Gail found she was standing in the sea, the ocean licking at her wound.

Kay had slipped the shell off her head and grinned. "Clean," she'd said, as she helped Gail out of the water. She'd half-carried Gail back up the beach to keep the sand out of the cut, and Gail had hopped on her one good foot, the shell still clutched in her hand.

For the rest of that day, Gail could feel the ghost of the pincers in her hands, like a haunting. It felt like this, the memory of something else in your body. Gail swallowed and stared at her hands. She was like a hermit crab now. A hermit crab without a shell: vulnerable and soft without her shadow.

Gail thought of Kay today, in her bed, staring out the window. She saw the flatness of her dark eyes, the way they looked through her and past her. Then Gail's breath caught in her throat. If other shadows could hold on to Gail, they could trap Kay as well. What if Kay had already been caught by one? Would she be able to remember who she was? Because she wasn't herself any more. She hadn't been for weeks.

Gail struggled to her feet. She needed to keep going. Anything could be happening at home.

"Wait up," Mhirran called after her, but Gail barely heard her. She ran, feet dodging shadows and rocks, until she saw a sliver of light ahead. Squeezing through the narrow crack, she stepped out of a craggy rock face into a forest, Mhirran close behind.

The ground was spongy with moss and rain. Clouds raced across the sky and the wind whipped at her cheeks, tugging at her hair.

"See!" Mhirran grinned, holding out her arms and spinning. "No one knows the caves better than me!"

Gail filled her lungs with a deep breath. It felt like breaking the surface of water. The air smelled of wood smoke and insect secrets. She put her hand to the bark of an old oak and felt the knots and gnarls of its trunk. In the silky light, Gail could see circles curling around a tree stump. She thought of the stalactites in the cave, and Francis. A bird's shriek sliced the air above them and Gail tensed.

Mhirran was already moving purposefully further into the forest. Her hands were splayed at her sides, fronds of fern and twigs handshaking her as she passed. Her orange hair felt too bright in the mossy green and her boots squeaked loudly as she walked. Gail stared after her. Something felt wrong.

"Mhirran," Gail called, running after her. "Wait. Where are we going?"

Mhirran turned. She looked surprised. "To my uncle's. We'll get food. I'm hungry, aren't you? It's okay, Francis will still be in the tunnel."

"Wait, stop. I can't just come to your uncle's. I need to find Kay's shadow."

Mhirran paused, her hand tightening around a fern. She looked around the forest uneasily. "Gail, we have to keep going. We'll get food at my uncle's, and maps, then we'll look for Kay's shadow."

"But you saw it, didn't you, Mhirran? You saw it!" The words burst out of Gail. "I have to find it *now*. It's getting further away all the time. You've got to try and remember. Did it go down this tunnel? Could it be out here in the woods?"

Mhirran's mouth curled in on itself, her gaze darting between Gail's knees. And when she looked up, Gail saw the truth billowing painfully in her eyes like a jellyfish bloom.

Chapter Seven

The forest quietened around the two girls, standing face to face. A blackbird trilled a few notes then gave up. The sky lowered itself onto their backs. Gail's eyes narrowed.

"Where did it go, Mhirran? Where did my sister's shadow go?"

But she already knew the answer. She could feel it like a stone in her stomach. Mhirran *had* seen Kay's shadow in the cavern. It must have gone right by her. "We weren't following it in our tunnel, were we, Mhirran?" Gail's jaw ached as she forced the words out. "Kay's shadow went down the other one. Where Francis went."

Mhirran squeezed handfuls of ferns between her fists as Gail walked towards her. Now that they were further inside the forest, the canopy closed darkly above them and the trees leaned into each other, branches groaning in the wind.

Gail frowned. It didn't make sense. "But why take me the wrong way?"

A sour taste prickled Gail's tongue and she felt sick as she remembered Mhirran's words to her brother. *You'll move quicker by yourself. You're bound to catch up with it that way.* Gail's eyes widened in horror.

"Your brother is trapping shadows," she said, aghast. Seeing the truth in Mhirran's half-step forward, her pleading eyes, Gail reeled backwards. "And you're helping him," she spat at the girl. "You kept me out of the way while he chased my sister's shadow. He's probably got her in his horrible mach—" Gail broke off, her fists pressed against her sides, eyes filled with the vampire squid funnel and tight rope of Francis's contraption. She remembered the flicker she saw as Mhirran checked the second of the machines: a trapped shadow. Gail shuddered and moved forward so she was inches from Mhirran's white face.

"Tell me where he is."

Mhirran's hair trembled and she backed away from Gail. "Wait, you're wrong. You've got it wrong," she stammered.

"TELL ME WHERE HE IS!" Gail's roar stretched around the forest, reverberating off trunks. Birds scattered from branches.

Mhirran's mouth opened and closed and her ears

stood out painfully red. She looked younger than ever as she turned to walk away into the trees.

Gail chased after her.

"Answer me, Mhirran! What will he do with Kay's shadow? Where will he take it?" Gasping for breath, Gail stopped, staring at Mhirran's retreating back through narrow eyes. "Why would you help him?" she asked, bitterly.

At that, Mhirran paused and turned, slowly. Her chin rose to meet Gail's gaze, and although her mouth quivered, her eyes blazed.

"Francis is my brother, Gail," Mhirran said, and the words were hard and shining, like diamonds. "But I was trying to help you. Just like I said."

"By getting me out of the way so Francis could get my sister's shadow?"

"Yes. By getting you out of the way." Mhirran's voice shook. Her face contorted as if it was struggling with something. "I'll help you get your sister's shadow back, Gail. I promise."

"Just tell me where it went. Tell me why Francis wants it and tell me what he's going to do with it."

"Gail, trust me—"

The pufferfish inside Gail exploded into painful spikes.

"Stop it!" Gail burst out. "Stop lying to me! How

can I trust you after what you've done? Tell me where he went, Mhirran. You talk all the time, but you don't ever say anything real. You talk about whistling and webs and stupid Morse code but you can't even tell me the truth. I thought you were different to Francis. But you're just like him." Her voice cracked and her face was hot with fury as she kicked at a log on the ground, scattering damp chunks of wood.

"I got us out of the tunnels, I'm trying to help you and I *don't* lie," Mhirran said, her hands balled into fists at her sides. "Yes, Francis collects shadows. But he also uses people who've lost their shadow. Like you, Gail. He wanted to use you. He was going after your sister's shadow and there was nothing we could have done to stop him. But I got *you* out his way, Gail. I made sure you came with me. I got you out of there."

Gail's mind whirled but somewhere deep down, she knew that what Mhirran was saying was true. Francis had been suddenly interested in her when he saw she had no shadow.

"I could have stopped him, Mhirran," she retorted, but doubt wobbled her voice. Francis was bigger than her, and he knew the tunnels. He'd have got her *and* Kay's shadow.

Mhirran shook her head and her voice grew stronger. "Do you remember when Francis said your name was strange for a girl without a shadow? You know why he said that, Gail? It's because you're not a gale, are you? You're not a storm gale, or a fresh gale, or even a moderate gale. Gales are fierce and strong – they can whip up huge, huge waves in the sea and bring them crashing down on the shore. You're angry but you're not strong, because strong people don't shout at people who try to help them. You're not a gale, you're more like…" Mhirran blew a raspberry in the air. "Like a breeze, like nothing." Her hands were shaking but her eyes still blazed. "People lose their shadows because they lose themselves. You've lost yourself, Gail. You can't cast a shadow if you're not really here."

Gail swallowed hard. Her hands shook and her head felt tight and dizzy, like she was somersaulting deeper and deeper underwater. She tried to breathe but Mhirran's words spun through her lungs, catching at her breath. *You're not a gale… Gales are fierce and strong… You're nothing… You're not really here.*

In her mind, she saw again the birthday cake that her dad had sent, the GALE in wobbly blue sweets on top. *On the night you were born, your screams were fiercer than the gale outside, so we called you Gail. We knew then that you were going to be braver than all of us.* Gail bit her lip. She wasn't brave or strong. She didn't want to be here. She wanted to be home. She wanted everything to be normal. The pufferfish inside her stomach shrank into a dull ache, but everything still hurt.

"And you know why I talk all the time, why I talk to you, Gail?" Mhirran was blinking hard. "Because I'm trying to get you back. I'm trying to reach the you that's disappeared."

Gail stared at her shoes, her cheeks aflame.

"But it's fine," Mhirran said quietly. "I'll stop now." And she turned away.

Gail began to step forward, and her mouth opened in the hope that it would say something right, for once, but she couldn't move. Her feet were stuck. She looked down and saw the dark, jagged shape of a tree's shadow seeping thickly around her shoes. *No. Please. Not now.*

Her throat constricted with fear. Mhirran was already moving out of sight.

A thunderous rumble sounded in the distance. For a moment, Gail remembered the storm warnings, though this didn't sound quite like a storm. Root shadows wound themselves tighter and tighter around her toes. Gail felt old, so old, and so tired. She pulled desperately at her feet, trying hard to think of herself, of who she was, but all she could see was Mhirran's distant, retreating back.

"Mhirran," she croaked, and the word stumbled

brokenly into the forest. "Mhirran," she called louder. "Mhirran!"

Mhirran turned back towards her. Gail saw her mouth move but she couldn't hear what she said. The thunder was upon them. Only it wasn't thunder at all. A herd of stampeding deer burst from between the trees. They smelled of salt and sweat and fur and their eyes were wide like rock pools in their faces. Gail took a quick sharp breath. Mhirran was right in the way as the deer hurtled towards them.

Trapped in the tree's shadow, unable to move, Gail shouted to the pale girl standing frozen in the deer's path. But the strangled cry was numbed amid the beating hooves of the deer as they flew by. Gail searched for Mhirran through the blur of tawny fur, but her head spun and she could see nothing but the stream of the herd, pulsing forwards.

And as the last of the animals hurtled past, Gail stared in horror at the empty space where Mhirran had been standing. A space that grew bigger and bigger as the forest noises settled and the tree's shadow tightened around her.

Chapter Eight

A crow screeched far overhead, and the trees leaned towards each other, whispering. A sharp wind prowled the forest, musty leaves thrown like damp, dark confetti. Gail fell to her knees inside the tree's shadow, her throat hoarse from yelling. She felt entirely and unmistakably like crying.

Mhirran was right. She wasn't a gale; she wasn't even a light breeze. Her shadow had gone, Kay's shadow had gone, and she'd turned against the one girl who'd said she wanted to help. Gail swallowed. Kay's shadow hadn't just gone. It had been taken. Trapped by a shadow collector.

Panic bubbled inside her as Gail recalled the greed in Francis's eyes, and she felt the tree's shadow grow around her feet. Her ankles felt gnarled and itchy with insects. Her knees creaked, and she shuddered from the faint tickle of leaves in her ears. Taking deep breaths, she reached into her bag and found the picture of Kay.

In the photo, her sister looked ridiculous. Paint was oozing in slimy green-and-yellow globs off her face, and she'd crossed her eyes and stuck out her tongue. Her tongue was sneeze-green with paint. Gail remembered that day. It was a Thursday afternoon and they should have been at school, but Angus had called Gail a *fat fishface* at lunchtime and Kay had found her, blotchy and beaten, crouched under the hand dryer in the girls' toilets. Gail blushed at the memory. They'd gone home early and painted each other's faces into fish ("This is more like a fishface," Kay had said, grinning) and eaten a whole jar of peanut butter with their fingers.

Gail ran a forefinger down the photo, following the curve of Kay's cheek. Kay had always been the strong one, not her. She remembered the time when she'd broken her arm and Kay had drawn twenty-three octopi on her cast so that she had all the arms she needed, and when Kay had spent hours explaining the tides because Gail was afraid of not knowing when the ocean would shift or shrink. She remembered when her sister had taken the blame the day Gail had turned their mum's umbrella into a jellyfish with pink tissue paper and superglue, and when she'd squeezed Gail's hand and distracted her with stories of marine biologist Asha de Vos while Gail had her first terrifying injection.

And she remembered one day after Kay had started sinking, when she had turned to Gail in the sticky silence, and said softly, "Do you remember the time we went swimming last October? We stayed in for ages and when we came out our lips and fingers were blue. You squeezed my hand and I couldn't feel anything at all." Gail had nodded and Kay stared at her own hand, flexing her fingers. "I feel like that now, Gail. Everything is numb. It's like I've been swimming for hours. But I don't know how to get out. I can't get out."

Gail had stiffened at Kay's words then. Kay was the strong one. She needed Kay to be the strong one. And so she had tightened her mouth and tapped at the window and shrugged and said nothing at all.

Twigs broke behind her. They crunched in a creature-like way. Gail held her breath; she slipped the photo back in her bag and tried once more to wrestle her feet from the tree's shadow. It was beginning to convince her that there were leaves growing from her nostrils and in between her teeth: Gail had to touch her face to check that there weren't. She tugged her hair behind her ears, and shifted her rucksack higher on her back.

Leaves crackled to her right, followed by the scuttling of insects disturbed.

"Hello?" Gail whispered. "Who's there?"

For the first time, she wondered why the deer had been running so fast. Perhaps something had spooked them in the forest...

Gail shrank her head into her jumper. She had to get out of the tree's shadow. *Who am I? Remember who I am.* But all she could see was Mhirran's pale face, and Kay, flexing her fingers sadly on her bed.

Caww. A crow burst upwards, startled into flight: something was moving in the forest. Gail froze. She could smell animal: damp fur and hunger. Every part of her body tensed. She squeezed her eyes shut, frantically racing through all the defences she knew: the octopus's spray of ink, the eel's organ regurgitation, the slime of the hagfish. She thought of the leafy seadragon's camouflage and the jellyfish's sting. And then she thought of Kay and the way she stared everybody down without any other kind of weapon at all. So Gail opened her eyes.

The eyes staring back at her were full of wilderness. Of hunts and hiding. Of exile and territory. They were full of night secrets and independence. They were coral-proud and luminous. They shone.

Gail's mouth opened and closed like a stranded fish. The cat was only an arm's length away. It stared at Gail, its thick, black-tipped tail twitching.

Once upon a time, Rin said that Miss said that

someone famous once said that to see yourself in the reflection of an animal's eye is to see yourself properly for the first time. Gail and Kay had spent that evening circling the goldfish bowl where Spot and Spots deftly avoided their eyes. They'd prodded the hamster awake and squinted and squashed their faces next to his, but his round black eyes showed nothing but shiny indifference. They'd used binoculars to stare at Mr Chopra's yellow-eyed cat, but it showed them its tail instead. And so they'd given up, deciding that Rin and Miss and the famous someone knew nothing about it at all.

But here in the forest, a tree's shadow curled around her feet and sunlight trickling through the leaves, Gail could see herself in the cat's eyes. She could see Kay in the shape of her own jaw and the curl of her hair but Gail's nose was smaller than Kay's, and her eyebrows were straighter and her cheeks twitched in different ways. She looked small and lost but distinctly like herself. Her seal-brown eyes stared back at her and her uncertain mouth straightened.

And as she stared at her own reflection, Gail felt something shift below her. The tree's shadow was loosening, each root rolling away. Gail's heartbeat thumped in her ears as the cat slowly blinked her reflection back again. In the cat's eyes, Gail looked braver than she felt. Her fringe spun above her forehead in dark coils and her nose was clustered with determined freckles.

She wiggled her cramped feet gently and flexed her fingers, while the cat casually yawned and licked a paw. Gail attempted a smile. She felt more solid somehow, like she knew where her edges were. And she knew what she had to do. She had to find Mhirran. Francis had caught Kay's shadow – the pufferfish in Gail's stomach prickled her ribs – and Mhirran would know where to find him. Gail took a deep breath.

Think.

She squeezed her eyes shut, recalling the pulsing beat of the herd flooding through the forest. *Like a tidal wave*, Gail thought. *A deep-sea current*. Gail blinked, her eyes tracing patterns in the muddy ground. No one can fight a current. You just have to swim with it.

So Gail half-stumbled, half-ran through the forest, following the trampled ferns and churned hoofprints of the deer. Mhirran must have gone in the same direction as the herd, taken up by the current of movement. "Mhirran?" she gasped out as she ran, but no one answered. Surely she couldn't be far? Gail urged her tired legs forward, then slipped and cried out as a splinter of bark caught in the soft skin of her thumb. As she paused to suck the sliver of wood from her hand, a shiver trickled down her spine and she froze. The forest felt suddenly alive. Goosepimples tickled her skin. Something slipped through the undergrowth in the corner of her eye. And there it was: a shadow the length of her arm, its darkness swimming and sliding like a reflection of the clouds rolling above. Gail gasped in recognition. It was like the shock of cold water, or the sudden sharpness of a stone in the soft pad of your foot. Her own shadow was watching her.

She gulped for air. What do you say to your own shadow?

Hi? How are you? (Why did you leave me?)

"Wait." She reached out an arm towards it. "Wait for me."

But the shadow slipped neatly over tree roots, rushing away from her reaching arms.

"No," Gail whispered. "Come back." Her tired voice fell into the wet undergrowth and she stumbled forward, a tight pain winding its way up through her ribs as she watched the dark blur of her shadow dart away between the trees. Gail bit her lip, stifling the urge to cry out. Then she dug her toes into the mud and pushed her hands deep into her pockets. Her shadow didn't matter. It couldn't matter. She had to find Kay's shadow now. She had to free it from Francis's machine.

She twisted her toe harder into a deer's hoofprint and tried to breathe out the hurt that ached through her, but the hairs on the back of her neck still crackled. The watchful feeling remained. She pushed her fringe back from her face, searching the woods. A pine cone creaked beneath her shoe. She turned slowly, her ears straining.

"Mhirran," Gail croaked, coaxing her voice from a dry throat. "Mhirran!" Her eyes scanned the forest for a flash of orange hair.

But it wasn't Mhirran who appeared from behind a large hollow tree stump, only metres from where Gail stood.

Chapter Nine

The boy was as startled as Gail, and he put his finger to his lips immediately. Gail stared at him, mouth agape. Weak sunlight slanted across his face. From the corner of his eye, curving round to his chin, the boy's black skin was pearly white. The shape looked almost like a crescent moon, and was matched by another pale patch on his forehead that curled in on itself like a shell. They gave his face the look of an atlas.

Gail swallowed. Her eyes slipped from his face, embarrassed, but then lifted again as the boy said: "You're Kay's sister."

It wasn't a question.

In the shocked silence, Gail's heartbeat thrummed against her ribs. She stepped closer.

"You know my sister?"

A half-smile twitched at the boy's cheeks. He had short dark hair and stood tall and straight as a pine, a rucksack straining at his shoulders.

"Yes," he whispered, nodding. "I know Kay."

"How?" Gail demanded loudly. "What are you doing here?"

The boy hissed at her to be quiet, looking uneasily behind him into the dense tangle of forest and gesturing her closer.

Gail scowled, but crossed over to crouch next to him beside the stump. Up close, the white patch above the boy's eye looked like the outline of the island.

"Why are we hiding?" Gail asked, quieter, the ground soaking into her knees. "And how do you know my sister?"

But the boy ignored her. His eyes were bright and burning with expectation. "Where's Kay? I've been leaving her messages, but I didn't hear... Did she tell you to come?"

Gail stared blankly at him.

"I'm Femi," the boy whispered. Then, leaning closer: "Did she tell you to find me?"

"No, I came by myself. I don't..." Gail frowned as the brightness in Femi's eyes went out. "Wait, why would she tell me to find you? Who...?" Gail looked at the boy, his long limbs tucked beneath him like origami. "It's you," she breathed out slowly. "*You* did the drawing. *You* left the map for her."

"You found it?" Femi looked relieved. "But where's Kay?"

Gail's face closed over. "I'm looking for her shadow," she said at last. Femi raised his eyebrows and Gail felt a spark of defiance rise in her. "That's why I'm here. I'm looking for Kay's shadow. It's been taken." It was almost true, she told herself. "What's the map for?"

"You're looking for her *shadow?*" he said in blunt disbelief.

Gail stared him down with narrowed eyes, her mouth set in a fierce line, and shifted as if to leave, but Femi pulled her back. "Okay." He shrugged half-apologetically and laughed. "If you say so, I believe you. Kay talked about you a lot." He paused, and Gail felt the words swoop through her, like the slow stroke of a turtle. "You're just like she said you were," he added, with a lopsided grin.

Gail scowled but before she could retort, a stream, of swearing from the bracken behind them broke the quiet.

Femi leaned quickly towards her, ignoring the question in her wide eyes. "I'll look out for her shadow. If it's here, I'll see it. I'm good at finding things." He paused and Gail saw his hand move deftly across the ground to his side. "Are you? Can you find things?" he asked her, and there was a strange urgency behind the words. "Use the map. There's something I need—"

"Femi, what you doing?" The voice was raw with impatience and Gail caught a glimpse of a boy striding out of the bracken before Femi pushed her inside the hollow of the rotting tree trunk.

"Got a stone in my shoe. Stopped to get it out, that's all." Femi rose to his feet, his voice steady and slow, designed to make peace.

"Sounded like you were talking to somebody. Are you talking to yourself now? Come on. Gus is way ahead. You've been hanging back all day, slowing us down. And you're the one who suggested this spot so we'd better find something."

"We'll find something, Euan. Trust me."

As he spoke, Femi turned slightly towards Gail and, so quickly she wasn't sure if she'd imagined it, he flicked his hand once, then twice, to the side.

Crouched inside the hollow, Gail could see Euan's pale skin glistening with sweat as he gestured to Femi to move past him. "You're taking us right across the island, Femi. If we don't find anything..."

Femi straightened his rucksack. "We will," he said lightly. "We'll find what we're looking for tomorrow. Let's walk another half hour then camp. Or if you've changed your mind, we can head back. It's a long way still and it's going to be a cold night."

Euan grunted and shook his head. "Let's go."

From where Gail hid, she could see the tightness of Femi's fingers as he held onto a branch. But he nodded and headed on with Euan close behind, blue sleeping bags bouncing against their rucksacks.

When she could no longer hear them, Gail breathed out, releasing the damp bark she'd been squeezing between her fingertips. She straightened cautiously and clambered out of the hollow, brushing lichen off her cheeks and woodlice from her knees. She stood for a moment, one hand on the trunk. Mushrooms dotted its slope like a staircase and their dark curves were speckled brown like Femi's eyes. He reminded her of Kay. He reminded her of Kay when she stood as far out as she could on the rocks at their beach, salt spray in her eyelashes and her arms stretched forward, her face turned to the wind. Afraid and fearless, all at once.

Gail shivered the memory away and the sounds of the forest settled around her. Above, a bird spun out a clicking tune that fell into a puddle of notes then grew again into a cascade. She knew she should keep moving, keep looking for Mhirran, forget about Femi. But she stayed there, by the tree trunk.

He knew Kay. He'd asked for her help.

Gail chewed her lip and looked to the right of the

stump, where Femi had gestured. She recalled the strange sweeping movement he'd made with his hand. *Can you find things?* She knelt down and flattened a fern to the side. Her mouth curled upwards as she saw what he'd done.

The shape of the island was drawn into the soil with a fingertip. Here was the north, where she'd come from. There was the harbour, marked with a deeper hole for the town. And here – she traced her finger across the ground – here at the south-west corner, where the island jutted out into a thin point, a cross was scored into the soil. Gail reached to pick out the pebble he'd placed in the centre of the cross. But as she drew it up, she realised it wasn't a pebble at all: a pearl shone dimly in the centre of her palm, milky as a moon and cold as betrayal.

Gail gasped. She pulled the mussel shell she'd found in the tunnel out of her coat pocket. Folding open the paper map, she looked from it to the map sketched on the ground, as Kay's voice bloomed inside her head: *Where did you find it, Gail? Who did you get it from?* It had been before summer, before everything had changed. Gail had found the shell on the way back from school, cast aside on the pavement, and had been shocked at her sister's anger, light flashing in her eyes. *Look at it. Can't you see what it is? It's a freshwater mussel shell.*

People are fishing and killing them here, on this island, to sell the pearls. They're being hunted to extinction, Gail. She'd taken the shell from Gail and her voice had softened in reverence. *This one was old, so much older than us. Maybe a hundred years.*

A blackbird trilled in the tree above her as Gail stared at the pearl, waiting for the knot inside her head to untangle. Her stomach churned in anger. They were pearl fishing, those boys, looking for freshwater mussels. And Femi was leading them.

Gail shook her head. It didn't make sense. It was illegal, so why would he leave her this map? Why would he show her where they were going?

The sharp cry of the blackbird startled Gail out of her thinking. Its song was straight and urgent and sounded almost like a whistle.

Whistle if you need me, that's what Mhirran had said, back in the tunnels.

Of course. Gail scrambled to her feet, tucking the pearl and shell back in her pocket. Taking a deep breath, she licked her cracked lips and tried to whistle. The air wobbled out. She tried again. This time, a faint sound glided away from her. The next was clear and sharp.

Gail waited, holding her breath. After a moment, she tried again, the whistle high and strong.

And this time, from not so far away, a tired high note came back to her.

Gail blinked. Had she imagined it? She whistled again, her ears straining for the response.

When it came, quieter this time, hot relief flooded through her. Mhirran would know what to do. She'd know where Francis was, where he'd taken Kay's shadow. She'd know about Femi. Gail hurried towards Mhirran's whistle, hope unfurling inside her, as she dodged branches and ducked beneath sweeps of conifer. And, there, like the tiny headlights of the pinecone fish, a flash of orange sparked in the corner of her eye.

Chapter Ten

An arm of bluish-green needles swept across Mhirran's cheek like a curtain. Her glasses were striped with dirt and one knee was drawn up to her chin. There were holes in her jeans and scarlet grazes beneath them. Her right hand was curled around her left wrist, which was red and swollen. When Gail gently nudged the orange fringe from her forehead, Mhirran's eyes were closed. Relief drained from Gail's body and, in its place, something cold and hard settled in her gut. She bit her lip against the painful squeeze of it.

"Mhirran," Gail whispered, touching her elbow. "Mhirran," she said again, louder, her heart beating in her ears.

At last, Mhirran stirred and Gail breathed out. "Where does it hurt? Is it your foot? Your wrist? Is it broken? What should I do?"

Mhirran twitched. It was a twitch that could have meant everything hurts or nothing hurts.

"I'm sorry, Mhirran," Gail began, "about what I said. It wasn't... I'm not... I think you're..." Gail took a deep breath, watching Mhirran's fingers flex on her injured wrist. Her fingers looked so small. Mhirran looked small. As if her chatter had made her seem bigger than she was.

Gail tilted her head. White clouds rolled across the sky and a cold breeze curled around her neck. Her stomach growled and she realised it must already be well past noon. What now? They could be miles away from Mhirran's uncle, miles from Francis and his machine, miles from Kay's shadow.

Mhirran's face was chalk-white, the freckles standing out like islands on her cheeks, and her breathing was shallow. It felt like she was a long way away. Wait, what had Mhirran said before? That she spoke to Gail to find her again...

Gail searched frantically through her mind for something to say. Then she remembered when she'd been so hurt and felt so clumsy after she'd broken her arm falling downstairs, and Kay had told her about the sunfish while she drew each octopus tentacle carefully on the cast. Gail smiled and cleared her throat.

"You know, Mhirran," she said, "there's a gigantic fish called the sunfish. They're silvery and clumsy and kind of like a circle. They weigh nearly five thousand pounds, which is, like, four-and-a-half times what a polar bear weighs. And they float in the ocean. Imagine that," she breathed. "A fish weighing more than a polar bear, swimming in the water. Some things are impossible," she said, "until you discover them."

Smiles, Gail learned, are luminescent. *Like fireflies*, she thought, as Mhirran's smile lit up the dim shade of the conifer. Then Mhirran coughed and spluttered and Gail gently hooked an arm around her back to lever her into a sitting position, leaning against the tree. As she shuffled Mhirran upright, Gail saw that the limpet, still clinging tightly to her boot, was brown with mud. She reached down and wiped the worst of it off with her sleeve. The limpet was a long way from home now. Just like her. She looked at the young girl sitting next to her. Just like Mhirran, too. Gail smoothed the hair back from her friend's face.

When Mhirran opened her eyes, she scanned the forest ground around them before turning to Gail.

"I saw it."

Gail froze. "You saw it. You saw Kay's shadow? Here? It got away?"

Mhirran shook her head and her mouth pinched as the movement nudged her wrist. "I saw *your* shadow, Gail. Right here. I'd fallen and tried to roll out the way of the deer and when I tried to get up, I saw it. It swept right by me and I tried to reach for it, but..." Mhirran closed her eyes again. "It was moving too fast."

"Are you sure it was mine?"

Mhirran grimaced. "It was yours, Gail. It wasn't hers."

"I saw it too," Gail said at last, trying to swallow her disappointment. The hurt she'd felt when she'd seen her shadow disappear rushed through her once more. "My shadow knew I was there and it left me again." She took a deep breath and eased the cold air slowly out through her teeth. "I wish it had been Kay's." She tightened her hand around a mulch of wet leaves. He'd got it. He'd got Kay's shadow.

Mhirran reached out a hand and curled one cold finger around Gail's thumb, like a seahorse anchoring itself in the ocean. "We'll get it back, Gail," she whispered, her voice tight. "I promise."

Gail stared at the young girl, glasses askew and lips edged with purple. Something turned inside her.

"It's okay, Mhirran," she said softly. "You don't have to."

Mhirran smiled then and her eyes shone like they had when Gail first met her, a strange girl with orange hair tapping Morse code deep inside a tunnel like the whole island might be listening.

"You don't mean that," Mhirran said.

Gail grinned in relief. "I need to find Francis, Mhirran," she said. "I need your help."

Then she frowned as Mhirran's seahorse finger tightened around her own. "You're freezing. Here." She rummaged in her rucksack for gloves and as she pulled them out, the photograph of Kay fell to the ground. Mhirran reached for it, wiping the mud-soaked edge gently on her sleeve.

"She looks just like you. Half you and half leafy seadragon." She smiled.

Gail blinked at Kay's green, glowing face. "I was painting her into a queen angelfish, not a leafy seadragon," she murmured. "Leafy seadragons camouflage too well, Kay always said. But she wanted to stand out." Gail frowned. "She never wanted to disappear." Her voice was edged with pride even as the words bit into her stomach. She tucked the photo deep into her bag, letting out a stifled cry as she retrieved two squashed sandwiches from its depths: "Here, I forgot about these." She passed one to Mhirran.

The wind blew pine needles into their hair and down their backs as they chewed, and Gail rubbed the prickle from her neck.

"Can you stand?"

Mhirran nodded and lurched to her feet. Gail pulled a scarf from her bag and wrapped it into an awkward sling around Mhirran's neck, gently lifting her wrist to her chest.

"Thanks for finding me, Gail," Mhirran said softly as Gail tied the knot at her shoulder.

Gail felt the words float inside her, bright like orange buoys. She squeezed her toes inside her shoes and straightened. "Where now?"

"If we find the river and follow it up past the waterfall," Mhirran said, "then my uncle's is just over the stones. Francis will be there," she added, avoiding Gail's eyes. "He always brings them home."

Gail's face tightened at Mhirran's words but she busied herself with her bag so Mhirran wouldn't see. Lifting it onto her back, she took a deep breath, then stepped three paces into the forest and closed her eyes. Kay used to say that even if Gail was spun a hundred times, she'd still be able to point to the sea. Gail would laugh and reply that on an island, the sea is in every direction. But Kay was right. It was like she could smell where the ocean was closest. River water was different, though. Her head ached from listening and her feet were numb from the cold. But she listened until she could hear, to her right, the faintest splash of running water.

Chapter Eleven

"It's so beautiful," Mhirran breathed as she stared wide-eyed at the pearl rolling in Gail's palm. It glinted like the river which swam through the forest alongside them.

Gail frowned at the pearl as she walked. It was cold in her hand, a small cold planet, but it glowed like the cat's eyes, luminous as the moon. Full of secrets. She closed her fist firmly around it and returned it to her pocket.

"It's bad," she said. "It's wrong what Femi's doing, killing mussels for their pearls." Her hand grazed the old empty shell in her pocket.

"And the map was the same as the one you found by Oyster Cave?" Mhirran asked as Gail steadied her on the uneven ground. Trees leaned over them, branches clicking like fingers, as they edged awkwardly along the riverbank.

"No, it was the whole island that he drew. He'd put a

cross on the southern tip, where the island comes out in that thin point, and that's where the pearl was. And when I looked at the map from the cave, the outline matched. So that's what the map shows, the sharp southern tip, where they're pearl fishing." Gail paused. "And he's leading them. That's what the other one – Euan – said. Femi's showing them the way. So why did he leave the map for Kay? She'd never have fished for pearls."

"Can I see it?"

The thin paper flapped in the wind as Gail handed it over, and Mhirran took it with her good arm, holding it inches from her nose to peer at it. They walked in silence for some minutes, the only sound the squelch of their shoes in the mud.

"It doesn't make sense," Mhirran said at last. "I've seen Femi in the caves sometimes. He was the first person I met down there, weeks ago. You were the second." She grinned at Gail. "But he's always by himself."

Mhirran's voice was soft, remembering. "He does the most amazing drawings. He was doing a leatherback sea turtle when I met him. They're so huge. He drew it twice as big as me. Did you know some sea turtles speak to each other? Everyone thought it was impossible, because they don't have vocal cords. But they do it. And the babies even talk from inside their shells. In hoots and clicks.

"Then after that I kept seeing him or his drawings. He did this sea lion and its whiskers were like my uncle's moustache, and one morning there was a whole reef of coral sketched down a tunnel from one end to the other. It must have taken him forever. And I saw the manta ray. He's not drawn that before. It was beautiful. Are you sure it was for Kay?"

Gail nodded. "I'm sure." She paused, feeling a decision wrap itself, kelp-like, around her. Her hand tightened around the shell in her pocket. "Mhirran, I'm going to come back," she said determinedly. "After we get Kay's shadow. I'm going to come back and follow him. What they're doing... It's not right and I don't understand it but..." The harsh ridges of the shell were rough in her palm. "...But maybe I can stop it."

Mhirran shot her a glance. For a second, Gail thought she saw something like relief flicker in her eyes. "Then I'll help too," she said. "You might need me. Did I tell you I can do bird calls and Morse code and semaphore?"

Gail rolled her eyes. "And speak Dolphin," she added, and Mhirran began a string of whistles and clicks, eyes winking at Gail to join in until the trees rattled with dolphin chatter and they were both clutching their stomachs and gasping for breath, their grins as wild as their voices.

"What's it like?" Mhirran asked suddenly, when she could speak again. "I mean…" She caught Gail's eye and reddened. "Where do you think it's going?" She glanced at Gail's feet.

Gail's fringe fell into her eyes and something cooled inside her. She watched Mhirran's shadow swing casually by her shoes and stared down at where her own should be. *What's it like?* The question rattled inside her, and the answer rose from all the hollow places where it ached. Lonely. *It's lonely*, she thought. *It's like being left behind.* First by her sister. Then by her shadow. Her eyes stung and she rubbed at them angrily.

She shrugged Mhirran's question away and urged her legs to go faster. "Cold," she said, forcing a tight smile. "My toes are cold."

By the time they reached the waterfall, Gail was exhausted. The clouds had cleared, and the river glistened in the sunlight, stones shining like eyes from its depths.

The water fell metres from where they stood. Rocks

stuck out like teeth around it and the ground sloped treacherously upwards. Gail struggled through the stones and gorse, her knees sinking into mud when she slipped. Mhirran followed slowly behind, her mouth a thin line of pain as her wrist jangled in its makeshift sling.

As soon as she bridged the slope, Gail clapped her hands over her ears. The water thundered inside her head and through her bones, crashing and churning her stomach. She fell to her knees, spray clinging to her eyelashes and dripping off her nose. The sound rolled and rolled inside her, over and over.

She was tired, so tired, and so far from home.

Gail crawled forward on her hands and knees, Mhirran still picking her way through the stones further behind. She just wanted to be out of the spray. Just somewhere she could curl up. So she could forget everything. Forget her shadow. Forget Francis. Forget Femi. Forget Kay's broken eyes. Just for a moment.

The water roared around her, thundering into the river in an explosion of white foam, and Gail dragged herself towards it, closer and closer, until she saw the ledge she was hoping for, and slipped into the dark space behind the waterfall.

It was like a dream. Or, Gail thought, it was like watching a film of a dream. Like the old projections Miss Flint showed in class. The water fell in a curtain in front of her. The stone ledge was narrow and Gail saw dark-green algae clinging to it, like the stripes in Kay's hair.

Meet me behind the waterfall. It was their code. They'd never been behind a waterfall before. Gail hadn't known that there were any waterfalls on the island, apart from the dribble on the way down to the beach. But they couldn't even fit a foot behind that one. *Meet me behind the waterfall.* They'd whispered it when they'd discovered something that had to be shared in secret, or when they were sad, or when their mum was tired and quiet, or their dad's friends lingered too long, and touched their hair while telling them that they were *just too cute.* Then Gail and Kay would retreat to their bedroom and crawl under the bed and pull the duvet over the edge and Kay would make waterfall noises sometimes, or Gail would.

"Meet me behind the waterfall." Gail whispered it softly now, as she curled into herself and forgot about Mhirran and her swollen wrist. Forgot about Femi and Francis.

"Meet me behind the waterfall."

She closed her eyes and, just like that, just as she

asked, there she was: Kay in a stripy swimsuit, aged nine and a half, staring at her with her cheeks puffed out and her eyebrows higher than her forehead.

Gail was sitting opposite her in the bath, counting. "Thirty-five, thirty-six, thirty-seven..." and on thirty-eight, Kay let out the breath with a spurt of laughter. Their nan was painting her own nails bright orange and dousing the girls with the shower at random intervals. They loved it when she arrived from Barbados, bringing instructions on how to treat a man o'war sting (with green pawpaw), and stories of flying fish and recipes for macaroni pie and conkies that put their mum's to shame.

"Forty-two, forty-three, forty-four, forty-five, forty-six. Forty-six!" Kay shouted as Gail gurgled her victory and grinned, her smile an equator going around the world and back again.

She'd always been able to hold her breath longer than Kay could. *Bigger lungs*, Kay always said, and prodded her in the chest with a mixture of pride and envy.

In bed, Gail would hold her breath and try to beat her own personal best. She read that the record for a mammal holding its breath underwater was the Cuvier's beaked whale at one hundred and thirty-seven minutes. Gail kept trying.

It was summer, that time in the bath. Gail

remembered the sunlight glancing through the window and their nan saying it was hurricane season back home while she painted Kay's nails green and Gail's salmon-pink. She said the hurricanes were worse than they'd ever been. That they were destroying people's homes. And that the coral reefs were dying. They'd listened to her, open-mouthed, small fires of outrage burning in their chests at what was happening to the Caribbean island, itching to fix it, with the water drying slowly on their skin.

And that evening, while Kay was brushing her teeth, their nan had taken Gail's hand and followed the fate lines along it and said, "The sea en' got no back door, Gail. Remember that when you're swimming. Remember that you can hold your breath longer than Kay."

Gail squeezed her eyes shut and pressed her knees into her stomach. Her head was filled with the deep, beautiful lines around her nan's eyes and Kay's finger prodding where her lungs would be and Gail, lying in bed when she was six years old, letting her nan's words roll around and out of her like water. Because why did she need to remember that she could hold her breath longer than Kay? Kay would always be stronger. She would always be there. She would always be swimming...

Chapter Twelve

"Gail!"

Water thundered around her ears.

"GAIL!"

It dripped down the rock onto her face.

"GAIL! GAIL!"

Gail forced her eyes open. Mhirran was on her knees at the edge of the ledge, her wrist held gingerly in front of her. Her face was so pale it looked green and her eyes were huge with worry.

"I thought you'd fallen in," she said. Pieces of her hair were being tugged inside the waterfall's curtain.

Gail untangled her arms and legs and shrugged. She hoped that the shrug said everything she couldn't say.

Mhirran leaned heavily against the dark rock. "We're close now." Her eyes were closed and her face was squeezed up as if she could stop the pain that way. "I used to come here with my mum."

For the first time, Gail realised that Mhirran had

never mentioned her parents. She called her uncle's house 'home'. The thundering of the waterfall and everything Gail didn't know about her swept between them.

Gail stared at Mhirran's sling and the torn holes of her jeans. She inched forward. "Mhirran, how long can you hold your breath for?"

Mhirran's face cracked into a faint smile. She shook her head slightly. "Not long. You?"

Gail sighed. "A long time," she said. *Longer than Kay.*

Water-soaked light cast slippery shadows onto Mhirran's face and caught in her orange hair so that, for a second, it looked like it was on fire.

"Did you know that the longest time a mammal has held its breath underwater is one hundred and thirty-seven minutes?" Mhirran asked.

Gail grinned and straightened. Gently, she helped Mhirran off the ledge.

"Yes," she murmured. "I knew that."

Mhirran was right; they were close. Once they'd clambered up the rocks by the falls and stumbled through a patch of heather they saw the stepping stones, which shone out of the river like the backs of dolphins breaching. And rising out of the trees, just over the water, a tentacle of smoke spinning and twisting upwards marked where Mhirran lived.

Gail gasped. "But we're *here*!" She was pointing to a thin slip of road just visible between the trees. "How are we *here*?"

On the other side of the road, she could make out the red smudge of a telephone box. Peeling and out of use, it has been turned into a miniature library by the islanders, and Gail had borrowed books from it more than once. It only took an hour to walk there on a path which curved around Ben Fiadhaich. Landmarks spun and shifted in Gail's mind as she realised she'd swung in an arc back towards the village, and a wash of relief flooded her. She was almost home.

It was late now. The light was trickling out of the sky and the trees reared tall around them as Gail crossed the last of the stepping stones. It must be gone six, and the lateness chewed at her insides. Her mum would be worried. She quickened her pace as she followed the swaying glimmer of light that marked Mhirran's house. The light flickered as it dipped behind tree trunks. Now Gail could see the building, and as she stopped to stare, she realised that the flickering light hadn't stopped when she had. It was moving. As if someone was holding it.

Mhirran saw him before Gail did. She pushed her beneath the thick spiky branches of a conifer, where they could crouch out of sight.

"Don't let him see you," she whispered as she clung to Gail's coat.

"But he's got her shadow," Gail hissed, straining against Mhirran's grip.

Francis wasn't so far ahead, his torch licking at the ground and his whole body arched forwards over it. He moved stealthily, picking his path as if cautious of frightening something or someone. When a bird crackled the branches of a nearby pine, he started and lurched towards the sound, his torchlight slicing the dim grey of the tree neatly open. Gail could feel Mhirran's breath warm and fast on her ear.

"Don't let him see you," Mhirran murmured again as Gail inched closer, the rustle of her coat loud in the silence. The pufferfish felt small and cold in her stomach, like a dropped penny, an empty wish. Suddenly Francis turned towards them, and she froze. The conifer was dense enough to hide them, but his torchlight crept close and they held their breaths as it passed and he carried on through the trees.

Mhirran interrupted the silence. "He's looking for us." Her voice was flat and hollow as she stared after her brother, and Gail glimpsed a flicker of pain across the young girl's face that had nothing to do with her wrist.

"He's looking for me," Gail corrected, as she watched him round the corner of the house, the shadow swallower a heavy bulk on his back. "Where will he take it?"

Mhirran scrunched her face up in answer. "It changes," she answered heavily. "Mostly he takes them to his room. Other times he uses the shed, or the garage." She winced. "It looks like he's going inside though."

Gail's mouth twisted. "I can't get Kay's shadow if he's there, Mhirran." She raised her eyebrows in a question and Mhirran nodded.

"I'll go first," Mhirran said. "I'll spin a story about how I lost you in the forest when I fell and hurt my wrist. I'll get him away from his room somehow. There's another door at the back," she said. "Head for that and I'll whistle when it's clear."

Gail followed slowly and crouched beneath a window as she waited. She grimaced as a blister burst on her heel, and pictured her journey across the island in her mind. A strange sweeping curve, when she'd been sure she was heading south. But she was almost home. And she'd take Kay's shadow with her.

She ducked at a sudden beat of wings above.

But when she looked up, it was just the wind slapping cardboard labels against four jars wedged onto the window sill. Each jar was half-filled with water. The one on the left was so murky Gail couldn't see through to the other side. The one on the right glinted. The labels were written in thick black pen:

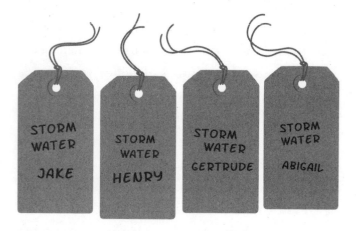

STORM WATER

JAKE

STORM WATER

HENRY

STORM WATER

GERTRUDE

STORM WATER

ABIGAIL

Gail frowned. The names sounded familiar but she couldn't puzzle out why.

The whistle curled around the edge of the house, long and low like the ocean's hum, startling Gail away from the jars. The all-clear. Half-crouched, she inched forward beside the wall, crunching along the short gravel drive where she bumped painfully into the handlebar of a bike. Every three steps, she'd stop and listen, her heartbeat high in her throat. But she heard nothing. It was as she reached for the back-door handle that a loud *thump* spun her around and she straightened, bracing herself to face Francis.

There was no one there.

Thump. A door clapped against the wall of a shed, opening and closing as the wind buffeted it *thump thump* onto the wood.

Gail hesitated. The wind had shifted. It had rhythm. It roared with the boom and whine of the ocean. And there was something in the air. Something salty. Gail's nostrils flared.

The shed door banged open and closed again. It swung on old hinges, makeshift and ramshackle. Paint peeled off it, though she could still make out the shape of a bird on the red door panels, pictured as if in flight.

Gail glanced back at the house. She knew she should slip inside now while Mhirran was distracting Francis. But she couldn't. It felt like there was a wave at her back, pushing her towards the shed. She had to see what was in there.

As she crept closer, something unnameable creeped into Gail's stomach, curling itself around the spikes of the pufferfish. Something cold and scaly. Something with teeth. Stepping inside, Gail squinted to make out anything in the gloom. The shed was cobwebbed and stacked with spades and forks and other tools, looped and swaddled by pieces of old blanket. But then she saw it. Low to the ground like a creature about to pounce. The shadow swallower. Francis had brought it here after all.

She fell to her knees, tearing at the straps, her hands trembling. She'd found it. She'd got Kay's shadow. She pushed the straps out of their holes, the leather flapping like tongues around her. Dust beat up in clouds as the chest shivered and jerked on the stone floor, a shadow shaking within.

"I'm here, Kay. I'll get you out." Gail's voice was ragged with effort as she tugged at the rope which slicked across the chest, binding it closed. Her fingers strained at the knot, dense and thick as her own fist. But it was no good. It only tightened against her efforts. Again and again, Gail felt the chest shudder against her body. Something was trying to get out.

Gail placed one hand on the flat top of it. "I know, Kay," she choked out, her voice thick. "I'm trying. I know." She yanked again at the rope, the roughness of it burning her palms in red stripes. But it didn't move. She couldn't open it. Eyes stinging, she fell back in despair and exhaustion.

"I can't. I can't do this. I need you..."

The footsteps were slow at first. Then they began

to hurry. Even as they drew closer, Gail knew they weren't Mhirran's. She froze, mouth agape. He'd find her here. He'd get her too. Then the chest shook again, like an earthquake was inside it, and Gail hesitated, torn between Francis and her sister's shadow.

But then she ran.

She ran from the *beat beat* of the chest. She ran from the salt sharpness of the sea and the trembling of Kay's shadow. She ran from the cold dark shed and flung herself towards the bike, jamming the helmet as far as she could over her hair.

"Hey! Wait! I've been looking—"

Gail ran past him, pushing the bike, then her feet were spinning on the pedals as she reached the road and could no longer hear him shouting behind her. She cycled until the only thing she could hear was the *thump* of her heart and the *beat beat* of the shadow-filled chest inside her skull.

Gail slowed to a halt and slumped forward on the handlebars, her chin resting on the lamp which spun eerie shadows into the road ahead of her. She'd run away. Just like Mhirran said. Just like Francis knew she would. She wasn't brave. She wasn't strong. She wasn't a gale. She'd run from her own sister's shadow. Her arms and legs jellied and everything hurt.

"It's over." Her words floated into the night like scraps of dark paper, torn and lost. "I can't do it."

And she cycled back down the road with moonlight glinting off her cheeks and the trees leaning away from her, like they knew everything she wasn't.

Chapter Thirteen

Soap suds melted on Gail's arms as she rinsed the plates slowly. Cake crumbs bobbed in the water. Behind her, Kay's chair scraped back and Gail heard her leave the room. Her mum called something after her but Gail didn't catch it. She let out a long slow breath and leaned down into the lukewarm water, her hand squeezing and releasing the sponge, over and over.

"I'll do that, honey."

Gail started at her mum's hand on her shoulder. She shrugged her away.

"It's okay."

"Gail." Her mum steered her gently from the sink. "It's your birthday. You don't have to do that."

Gail dried her hands and sat back at the table. A yellow stain marked where Kay had dripped curry sauce and smudged it with her elbow. Her mum had cooked so much there were piles of leftovers on the side. Like her dad was still here to eat his portion.

Kay had sat opposite Gail, her head low so her hair swung over her eyes. She'd asked Gail how her day had been in the clipped, polite tone of a stranger, and nodded at her mum's comments, pushing sauce in circles around her plate. And Gail had avoided her questions, chewed down her food, and tried to put smiles into all the lies she told her mum about Rin and the fun she'd had on her birthday. Her mouth tasted sour and her head hurt. And over the crackling silence between her and Kay, her mum had talked and talked as if that would fix everything. As if everything would be okay as long as she didn't stop talking, as long as the silence was kept away. But it never went away. It just grew and grew between them. And into the silence, the *beat beat* of Kay's shadow trapped inside the box sounded inside Gail's mind like her own heartbeat.

Gail stared at her mum's back, leaning over the sink.

"I miss her." The words fell out of her before she realised she'd said them. They grew in the room until she was sure they'd burst.

Her mum turned. Gail saw the tea towel squeeze and stretch in her hands. "Oh honey." And Gail knew what she was going to say. "I know you do. But..." Her mum's eyes glimmered and Gail noticed for the first time how the dark glow had faded from her cheeks and the lines had deepened around her mouth. She walked over and stroked Gail's fringe gently away from her forehead.

"Gail. She hasn't gone anywhere."

But Gail shrugged her touch away. It wasn't true. Kay *had* gone. She'd left her.

Gail turned from the liquid worry in her mum's eyes. The pufferfish prickled her stomach as she stormed upstairs. No one understood. She needed Kay to come back. She *needed* her. On her own she was helpless. How could she save Kay from sinking when she couldn't swim by herself?

She would have walked straight past if her eye hadn't been caught by the drawing. A sketch of a hawksbill turtle, inky brushstrokes carefully marking its narrow beak and overlapping scales. It was tacked to Kay's bedroom wall, near her door. Gail had never thought to ask where she got it from, but now she noted the **F** scrawled in the corner and her eyes widened.

"Did Fem—?" she began to ask as she pushed open the door. But then she saw her.

Kay was standing by the window, staring at the grey blank wall of the newsagent. Her arms were wrapped close around her body, as if to hold something in, or out. And she was crying. It was the first time Gail had seen her cry in years.

"A storm's coming," Kay said softly, as if to herself.

Gail swallowed, her fingers tightening on the door.

Kay's voice was wet and tired. "We were going to find the Storm Sisters at the next storm. Don't you remember?"

Gail nodded, though Kay didn't see it. At the place where the two giants joined, a hollow had formed and it was said that you could hide inside the Sisters during a storm, right on the edge of the island, and hear it roar and rage around you without getting a drop of rain on your head. They said at times like that, it was the safest place to be. It had been Kay's idea to find them, to hide inside the rock through the next storm.

Kay turned, wiping her cheeks.

Gail opened her mouth to say something, but nothing came out. She stood there with her mouth hanging open and her sister crying and all she could think of was Kay's shadow, trembling inside the chest.

"I'm sorry about the poster," she said at last.

Kay nodded and sat on the edge of her bed. She looked slowly from Gail's feet to her own, and a burn heated Gail's cheeks and pricked her ears. She'd failed. She stared hard at her own feet in accusation. The carpet was old and blue, and Gail scrunched her toes into the itch of it. When they were younger, they used to play a game where the carpet was the ocean and they had to step on different objects to reach the door without drowning, or the sea monsters would get them. Gail looked across the carpet to her sister. It felt like the whole ocean was between them now. Miles of deep, deep water. Her feet stopped at the edge of Kay's room and she couldn't make herself step inside. She'd never felt so far away from her.

Then Kay spoke, and it was as if she'd read Gail's mind. Her voice was so low, Gail could barely hear it. "Do you remember when we'd make this whole carpet the ocean? The North Atlantic, miles and miles of it, swimming with sea turtles and manatees and butterflyfish and striped dolphins and all the things that bite and spike and sting." Gail held her breath at the soft awe in Kay's voice. "All that water. So alive." Kay uncurled one foot from beneath her and swung her leg over the side of the bed. "The whole carpet was the ocean and we'd have to get across it without getting wet, without touching it. So the lionfish didn't get us, or the tiger sharks." Kay drew one toe across the carpet as if she was dipping her foot in the water.

A cautious smile crept onto Gail's face. "You always fell in," she said. "You said you weren't afraid of them. You wanted to swim with the whales."

Something flickered across Kay's face. A ghost of a ghost of a smile. Gail swallowed and stretched out one foot over the doorway, her toe brushing the blue carpet, and, just for one moment, they both had their feet in the same ocean. And in that second, something slow rippled between them. Something huge and magical and alive, swimming just beneath the surface. Like the ancient trombone of a whale's song, calling out across the depths. Gail glanced at her sister and their eyes met and she knew they both heard it, deep and aching and beautiful. The song shook her bones and fizzed through her hair. Gail felt determination rise through her like a storm.

"I'll get it back, Kay," she said, the words tumbling out of her. "I promise."

Chapter Fourteen

It was still dark outside when Gail woke the next morning and slipped on her boots. Her rucksack was packed with apples and biscuits, and the mussel shell and pearl jangled in her pocket. Last night, she'd hunted for something to cut the rope round the shadow swallower and now a pair of sharp scissors were wedged tightly between her extra socks and a bottle of water. Kay and her mum were still asleep, and she stepped on the edges of the stairs so as not to waken them. "This time," she promised the silent house, "I won't come back without it."

Ben Fiadhaich was capped in a blur of cloud and the road was empty of cars as Gail pedalled out of the village towards Mhirran's. The wind had risen in the night and it pushed against her as she cycled, her knees aching from the strain. When she reached the house, dawn was pinking the sky and Gail could see that there was already a light on in an upper window.

She held her breath and watched it, but couldn't make out anyone moving. Was Mhirran awake? Her heart sank. Or Francis?

On the gravel driveway, every footstep she took crunched loudly and Gail winced as she leaned the bike against the wall and inched towards the shed. The bird painted on the door was just visible in the early light; Gail's breath was thick in her throat as she pushed it open. But when she stepped inside, the wooden chest had gone.

Gail stared at the empty space, willing it to appear. She was ready. She could cut the rope. How could it have gone? Then she heard the brittle crack of twigs and the brush of leaves and spun towards the sound. Someone was moving down the path that led from the house into the woods. She could see their silhouette against the growing light. An odd hunched shape. It was Francis. And he was carrying the shadow swallower on his back.

Gail hurried after him without thinking. He was already moving fast away from her: there was no time to tell Mhirran. He was walking steadily downhill, into the trees, which clutched at each other with long finger-like branches. The night crouched in the woods as if hiding from the dawn, spinning its own eerie noises in Gail's ears, and her palms prickled as she hastened after him. Out of breath and tense with fear, she soon gave up trying to be quiet.

When Francis reached a wide flat loch and finally stopped, the sun was almost risen. Gail hung back at the edge of a forest clearing, seeing the water glow an eerie blue like the underside of a sea swallow. The wind tiptoed ripples across it and the first gleam of the sun licked at its edge.

Gail watched as Francis straightened then strode on towards the loch, the chest creaking on his back. She could feel the pull of the shadow swallower, even from here. She inched closer, and her eyes widened as she saw that Francis was walking towards an old woman, perched on a low flat stone.

Wrapped in a dark cloak, the old woman sat with one toe dangling in the water. She was knitting and her needles were *click-clicking* like an animal chewing on the night. She looked up at Francis's approach and smiled. Her smile was sharp and hard like a tooth. Between the knitting needles, tiny lightning bolts flashed and burned.

Gail stared. The woman's face was full of shadows. Not *in* shadow exactly, it was more like there were shadows drifting between the folds and wrinkles of her face, like thunderclouds gathering. Her hair was plastered to her scalp, and her cloak was weighed down with water, though it wasn't raining.

Gail stepped forward, out from the shelter of the trees. She couldn't help herself. There was something horribly magnetic about the woman. Something darkly fascinating, like a river overflowing, and Gail's nostrils flared at the metallic taste of thunderstorms in the air.

Francis was standing metres from the woman. Gail could see he was talking to her but couldn't hear what he was saying. Every now and then, he would gesture to the woman's cloak, thick and close around her, and she'd suck her teeth and tap the needles and her eyebrows would dart to the shadow swallower on Francis's back.

Finally, she nodded.

Gail froze as Francis turned around. She was clearly visible, halfway between the loch's edge and the trees. But he wasn't looking. He'd turned to pull the shadow swallower from his back and place it on the ground a short distance from where the woman continued knitting. Gail inched backwards but stopped when she saw that Francis was opening the chest. The rope was already flung on the ground and he was loosening the final buckle. Why? Was he giving Kay's shadow to the woman?

Gail heard the sound before she realised it was her own throat making it. A fierce cry edged with fear, as she hurtled forward, calling to Kay's shadow to run. *Run, run and escape!* But before Francis had time to react, the old woman had jumped neatly from the stone, and as soon as both her feet were off the ground, a stream of dark shadows poured from her cloak like thunderclouds rolling across the sky. The shadows streamed towards the chest, and Gail stumbled to the side, afraid of the smoke-like tendrils that reached out from the swirling mass.

It was then that she saw a shape drift away from the rest, and her heart leapt up in recognition. One shadow, swirling and rippling across the ground until, for one moment, it formed the shape of a huge manta ray, its fins moving like wings over the earth. Gail held her breath. *A flying swim*, Kay called it. Kay watched them in documentaries with her mouth half-open and her eyes glistening. Over and over again. Then she'd tell Gail for the hundredth time about the way manta rays would leap out of the water, almost nine feet up, and nobody knew why. She'd rewind the documentary to the part where it showed them leaping and her feet would twitch, and Gail would watch Kay watching the rays and be invincibly happy.

The shadow shifted, curling away from Francis, and Gail raced towards it. It wasn't a manta ray any more. The silky darkness grew and stretched as it swept towards the loch, until at last the familiar frizz of her sister's hair fanned out from the shadow's edges and Gail felt something bright as a butterflyfish light up inside her.

Kay's shadow had escaped.

Chapter Fifteen

Gail ran after Kay's shadow, hurtling past Francis and the old woman. Panting, she raced towards it as the shadow streamed closer to the loch, moving away from her.

"Wait!"

Gail leaped forward, and the tips of her shoes just touched the soft edges of the shadow. She gasped in relief, looking down into the shifting darkness, but her breath faltered in her lungs. She'd reached Kay's shadow but it felt all wrong. It writhed at her feet, trying to break free. She could feel the urgent tug of it, the purpose. Why was it pulling away?

Gail grit her teeth. She had to hold it. But how?

She knelt down inside it, her hands flat within the shadow's grey swirls, cold soil pressed against her knees. She remembered how she'd escaped the rock-shadow in the cave, when the tunnel had echoed her name back to her. And the time she was trapped in the tree-shadow she'd recognised herself in the cat's glowing eyes.

What if all I need to do is to remember Kay? To remember her so much that she's everything I'm thinking about? Gail squeezed her eyes shut and dived towards the first memory that came to her.

It was night. They were in Kay's bedroom. Kay was sitting up against the wall with the bedcovers by her feet. Her eyes were empty, like someone had turned them upside down and rinsed them out. Gail couldn't look at them. The silence was an eel in the room, sliding between them. Kay was refusing to come down to dinner. Her face was as grey and blank as the wall of the newsagent and with everything Gail said, she drew further and further away. The pufferfish grew and grew inside Gail's stomach until all the helplessness and anger burst out of her. *Get out of bed, Kay! There's nothing wrong with you. What about Mum? What about me? What about me, Kay?*

"No," Gail whispered. Not that memory... She could see Kay's shadow pulling further away from her. Gail pressed down into it, squeezing her eyes shut in concentration, trying to hold it close. Another memory, any other one.

The next was from before Kay's sinking. They were swimming. It was early, so early the birds were just shuffling into song. The water was dark and bitter cold and Kay's lips were blue as she backstroked towards Lighthouse Rock. The rock was small, only a metre across, and it didn't have a lighthouse. Kay had called it Lighthouse Rock because she said that when Gail stood on it, she lit up the ocean. Gail had squirmed at her words and made a sick-face with her tongue, but her fingertips had tingled with a sudden warmth and the name for the rock had stuck.

Kay had stood on Lighthouse Rock on one leg, spinning and daring Gail to join her. She'd laughed as she spun, her mouth open wide, and it was so long now since Gail had seen her laughing that the memory stopped and trembled uncertainly, and in that frozen moment, something pulled at the shadow, ripping up the ocean and the rock and Kay's bright smile, wrenching it from her.

Gail forced her eyes open.

Francis was squatting on the ground close by. His sleeves were rolled up, and next to him the shadow swallower was eating the old woman's swirling streaming shadows as if they were sweets. Liquorice laces.

Gail gulped for air. "No," she cried out. "Stop it!" She tried to hold on to the memory, she tried to hold on to Kay's shadow. But the funnel sucked it towards the chest with the others and Gail could do nothing to save it.

"Francis!" she screamed. "She's my sister!"

But Francis didn't flinch as his machine swallowed the flailing darkness of Kay's shadow, trapping it once more.

Chapter Sixteen

The loch glowed with the dawn, trees danced in the wind and the old woman was nowhere to be seen. A leaf fell onto Gail's face, and the sun rose higher and higher. It was too pretty for right now, for how this felt. Anything would be.

The water lapped against the ground like a mistake. Gail had found her sister's shadow and lost it in the same breath. And in that memory, Kay spinning on Lighthouse Rock, she'd felt closer to her sister than she'd let herself feel for a long time.

Francis's voice sounded like a chiselled ice cube behind her. "Who would have thought," he said, "that small, shadowless Gail would do some shadow experimenting of her own. Did you want to try out a new shadow, since yours has gone... missing? You should have asked me for help, Gail, if that's what you had in mind. I am," he paused, "*particularly* qualified in this area."

Gail finched at his words. "I wasn't experimenting. I was trying to get my sister's shadow back. Let her go, Francis."

Francis sat down across from her, stroking the canvas funnel of the shadow swallower by his side. "But what about the others? What about all those lost, hungry shadows that Gertrude released? Would you like those, too? Because if I open this up, they'll be looking for something to hold on to. Someone without a shadow of her own," he sneered.

Gail drew a quick breath. "What are they?" Her voice trembled.

"Storm shadows," Francis said, and there was a tight edge to his voice. "Don't you remember Storm Gertrude? She was so angry. And so loud. She wreaked havoc. Power cuts and flooding and gale-force winds."

Gail's mouth fell open. "That old woman. She was a storm?"

Francis raised his eyebrows. "I thought you might have got that far already, Gail. Gertrude is... what remains after the storm. My uncle has a misplaced obsession with these creatures. He thinks that so many storms end up on this island because of its wind and tide patterns. And when we name storms, we give them a shape. Gertrude, Henry, Imogen."

Gail recalled the storm-water jars on the window sill, the name of each storm written on the labels.

Francis opened his mouth to go on, then hesitated and, for a second, Gail saw a dark cloud pass over his face. "These storms destroy everything that they can. Everything that they can hurt, they will hurt."

Gail stared. Were his eyes glistening?

Before she could be sure, Francis took a deep breath, blinked and continued. "As the storm passes through, it gathers shadows in their hundreds. These are the shadows of everything that is killed or broken or hurt in the storm. Gertrude gathered many shadows," Francis finished sourly. "As you saw."

Gail shivered. She'd got it wrong. He hadn't been giving Kay's shadow to the old woman. "You were taking them from her," she realised slowly.

Francis frowned. "She let me have them," he corrected. "I've been looking for some storm shadows for a long time. Two shadows. A long, long time..." Francis's voice trailed away and his hands balled into fists so tight his knuckles turned white. His face was pale and his eyes looked beyond her, dark and dangerous as black ice.

"But you've got so many now," she stammered, fear cracking her voice. "You don't need Kay's. You've got so many."

"I haven't found them yet, those two shadows," he continued quietly, ignoring her. "While I've been looking, I've tweaked and nipped and shaped and worked on something quite special." He smiled and Gail's stomach turned. She risked a glance behind her but there was no one else around. "And now I meet you, a shadowless girl looking for her sister's shadow, and I think that this could be interesting." His eyes flashed. "Now I shall investigate shadow loyalties: blood ties and family bonds. It's the next step."

Gail felt her palms itch with sweat. *Shadow loyalties? Blood ties?* What did he mean?

"And didn't you say..." Francis's hand drifted to the chest and lingered there. "Didn't you just say that your sister's shadow was in here?"

Gail recoiled from the slither of his voice. What was he going to do?

If she was a mimic octopus, now would be the time to mimic a sea snake. She would slip into a hole in the seabed and only let two of her tentacles curve through the water looking like a venomous snake. If she was a sea cucumber, she would eject her intestines and other organs to dazzle and distract the enemy. But she wasn't either of these. She was small and afraid and all she could do was freeze her face so that her mouth wasn't giving anything away.

But of course that gave everything away.

Francis's smile stung of satisfaction and Gail squirmed from it, readying to run even as she knew he'd catch her. As she moved, her foot knocked against a jar that Francis had leant beside the shadow swallower.

"What's this?"

Something tremored at the corner of Francis's mouth and Gail knew immediately that she'd said the wrong thing. Anticipation shivered across his features as he reached for the jar.

"This? This is something I've been working on for some time now. All I needed was someone without a shadow. And now it's finally ready." He turned the lid and his face was all edges as he grinned. "And here you are. You're not scared of heights, are you, Gail?"

Chapter Seventeen

Two blurred bird shadows shot out of the jar as if their tail feathers were on fire. They were like winged tornadoes, all darkness and beak, and they hurtled towards Gail, pecking at her cheeks, at her neck, at the soft skin behind her knee. Then, as Francis clapped his hands, their claws took hold of her and she was being lifted higher and higher and higher in a frenzy of flight.

Gail had nothing to hold on to. She was flipping and rolling and twisting as their dark wings moved against the sky. She squeezed her eyes shut. Her head spun and she felt horribly sick. Yes, she was afraid of heights, but she was more afraid of flying shadows. Shadows stayed on the ground. Bird shadows, aeroplane shadows, the shadows of clouds: they all floated along the ground. What had Francis done to these shadows to make them fly? Where were they taking her?

The wind bit Gail's face and fingers and she retched. She risked opening her eyes, then wished she hadn't. She was far above the loch – it glowed like a stranded jellyfish in the forest – and the trees stretched out, back towards the caves, and on towards the south of the island. And there, way off, was the southern pointed tip, and the sea, fierce and fin-grey, crashing against the jagged cliffs.

One of the bird shadows pulled at her feet, the other pulled her arm, lurching her upwards. They were climbing higher and higher, as if it was the only place they knew where to go. The loch blinked beneath Gail and the island shrank.

Krrrrrrhuh Krrrrrrrhuh. A sharp clear trill rang out from somewhere below her. It was a high note, rising then falling in a chatter to end in a short trumpet call. It came again, piercingly clear, raising goose-pimples on Gail's skin. The shadow at Gail's arm hesitated, its head cocked towards the call. *Krrrrrrhuh Krrrrrrrhuh.*

Then the bird's wings folded and, abandoning Gail, it plummeted like an arrow down towards the sound.

Gail gasped. A wave of sickness swept through her as she jerked upside down, the shadow at her feet struggling with the extra weight. Was Francis calling the shadows back? She'd fall hundreds of feet to the ground. She was already falling. The lone shadow was beating brokenly against their descent but it wasn't strong enough. Wind pummelled Gail's cheeks and the breath was torn from her lungs. She could see the mangle of branches below her in the forest growing closer. Each tree bristled with needles. She tensed against the call that she knew was coming.

"Don't drop me now," she whispered to the shadow.

Krrrrrrhuh Krrrrrrrhuh.

Gail could see the fir cones on the trees beneath her. "Don't let go." Blood pounded in her ears.

Krrrrrrrhuh Krrrrrrrhuh.

The shadow didn't let go. It was flying her towards the bird call, but it was struggling. They were crossing the loch now; it grew fatter and wider beneath them, but the shadow was hardly moving its wings. Gail could feel its exhaustion numb her, deadening her flailing limbs.

When the cry came again, high and magnificent and somehow familiar, they were in freefall.

Gail didn't expect time to slow down just because that's what people said about falling, but it did. It was like when Sylvia pushed her off the top diving board and she plummeted for so long she'd already planned her revenge by the time she hit the pool.

She watched the water ripple and wait for her, and she saw, beyond Grimloch Woods, at the edge of her vision, a small rucksacked figure: Femi. He was walking behind two others. And, before that, on a boulder at the edge of the forest, she could see a bright white shape. A drawing. If she could only make out what it was—

When she hit the loch, the water was so cold it had spikes, and her body ached from the force of the drop. Bubbles popped in her ears and she spun to right herself, gasping for air. She could feel a current tugging at her feet. Gail panicked. All she could think about was when she was seven and she'd almost drowned. She'd been knocked over by a wave and somersaulted too many times to know which way was up. How had she got out then? Her arms thrashed and she kicked her feet helplessly towards dry land. It was so far away. Then she remembered: Kay had been there. Kay had held her and pulled her out.

Gail's eyes stung and she swallowed more water. She had never swum without Kay before.

She had never swum...

She had never...

She had...

Strong arms reached under her armpits and heaved her towards the shore. Gail gagged and coughed out water, feeling solid ground beneath her knees. She pressed her forehead to the damp soil, gulping for air.

The loch dripped from her nose and stuck the curls of her hair to her neck. Her clothes clung to her body and she shivered uncontrollably.

Gail rubbed the water out of her eyes and looked up. It wasn't Francis.

The boy didn't look much older than Femi, and he had the same shifting shadowy face as Gertrude. He was awkwardly perched on a low slab of rock, squeezing water out of his pockets. His clothes were full of pockets. He was wearing dark dungarees which wrinkled around his knees and flapped in the wind whipping around him. On each leg there were pockets attached to pockets, and each seemed to have a different fastening in place of a button. They jangled in the rising wind: shells and acorns, sea glass and seeds. Beneath the dungarees he wore a brown prickly jumper that bulged into odd shapes and sagged at the elbows. It looked like a doormat.

Under a mass of black hair, his eyes were shy and serious and his mouth hovered between a smile and a frown. The breeze that twisted around him zigzagged through his hair and puffed out his sleeves. Gail swallowed.

"Hi," he said eventually, holding out a damp and slightly shaking hand. "I'm Jake." Then, after a moment's thinking, he added, "That must have hurt."

Gail grimaced as she rolled her shoulder and twisted around to the loch, beads of water dripping from her. "What happened?" Then she realised that his last words weren't directed at her. She followed his gaze towards the huddled tangle of bird shadow still trembling at her feet.

"Urgh! Get off me!" Gail kicked her soggy shoes against the ground as if she could scrape the shadow off.

"Hey!" Jake pulled at her arm. "It's frightened."

"So am I!" Gail retorted. "Didn't you see what they did to me?"

Jake pointed across the loch to a thin figure marching into the forest with the wooden chest strapped to his back. "Francis did that to you," he said. "Not them."

Gail's eyes widened as another figure, with bright orange hair, slipped from the trees and followed a few steps behind Francis as he dipped beneath the forest's canopy. For one second, Gail was sure Mhirran looked back and saw them, but when Gail raised her hand to wave, she'd already gone.

"Mhirran?" she breathed. Where was she...? Gail tried to struggle to her feet; Jake held her back.

"Get OFF me!" Gail shoved Jake's arm away. "He's got my sister's shadow in that chest. I'm not going to let him do anything to it."

But as Gail pushed against the ground, her legs

swayed beneath her and she collapsed against the rock. The bird shadow clung to her tightly, its exhaustion pricking her muscles, numbing her mind and unravelling her determination. She closed her eyes and tried to remember her own reflection in the cat's eyes, but when she opened them the bird was still there.

"It's the shadow." Jake's voice was soft.

Gail stared at it trembling in a silky scribble on the sand.

"It's too sick to leave you and too weak to let you go. Bird shadows aren't meant to fly. Francis has been working on these for weeks, trying to give them flight. It's taken its toll on them."

Gail rubbed water from her cheek angrily. "I don't understand any of it! Why did he make them take me, and then call them back so they dropped me in the water? What is he doing?"

"Francis made the birds lift you, but he didn't call them back," Jake said.

"What?"

"It was his sister. I don't think she meant for them to drop you; she called them down. She was trying to help you."

"Mhirran?" Gail stared at him. Words echoed in her mind. *Did I tell you I can do bird calls and Morse code and semaphore?* "It was Mhirran? You know her?"

Jake nodded and a cautious smile grew on his face.

"Me too," Gail said, as a shoot of warmth wrapped itself around her stomach.

She looked up at Jake. The wind that surrounded him whipped up his sleeve and clouds shifted across his face. His pockets moved with a mind of their own, swelling and shrinking as the shadows fidgeted inside them. Gail knew he was a storm, just like Gertrude. Francis's words slinked inside her head: *These storms destroy everything that they can.* She bit her lip.

But he knew Mhirran.

Gail watched as Jake knelt down and brushed his fingers across the shadow trembling at her foot. His touch was tender. Gail swallowed.

"Will you help it?" she asked. "You said it was sick. If it gets better, I might feel stronger too. Can you fix the bird so I can make it let go? So I can follow Francis and get my sister's shadow back?"

Jake didn't answer at first. He got up and walked among the trees, collecting handfuls of twigs and broken branches. "How do you make a shadow stronger?" he asked, as he piled the wood on the bare dirt near Gail.

She shook her head.

"Light." Jake grinned.

Chapter Eighteen

Flames crackled and spat in the fire. Gail sat with her back towards it, twisting round so that half her face was red with heat.

At her feet, the bird's shadow grew slowly thicker and darker in the bright glow, its feathers fluttering like the fire. Clouds gathered thunder-grey, throwing dense veils over the sun. Gail had forgotten about the storm warnings. There was an electricity in the air, as if the sky had been twisted tight, then plucked like a guitar string. Gail's hair flew around her ears as she chewed on an apple from her rucksack. Though her face was hot, her feet were still cold.

Jake didn't speak much. When he did, his eyes fidgeted but the words were slow and calm. He'd said, as he built the fire, that Mhirran would come and find them. She knew where they were. He said she'd tell them where Francis had taken Kay's shadow. He said they had to wait for her. Gail didn't know how he could be so sure.

"What kind of bird is this?" Gail asked.

Jake glanced at the shadow. "A storm petrel."

"I think I've seen it somewhere," Gail murmured. "Not the bird itself, but..." She blinked. "It was painted onto the shed door at Mhirran's."

Jake nodded and Gail shuffled closer to the fire. "The shadow's getting stronger. I feel like I'm growing feathers." She grimaced. "How do you stand it? You must have hundreds of shadows in those pockets. Can't you get rid of them?"

Jake squatted on the ground. His mouth was lopsided as he shrugged. "No," he said simply. "Unless I found someone without a shadow, who could take them, or I gave them to Francis, like Gertrude does." He glanced at Gail. "But I'd never do that. I did this to them, so..." He looked away. "I owe them something."

Gail bit her lip, and tried to remember what stories she'd heard of the storm called Jake. How much damage did he cause? "Do you have to be so bad?" she ventured. "Mum says the storms are getting worse."

Jake stared at her. "We don't want to. But the air is changing. You're changing it," he said, stirring up the fire with a stick.

Gail tossed away the apple core and stared at the bird's shadow quivering at her feet. Her arms tingled and she could almost feel feathers flattening across her scalp. It frightened her.

"Remember who I am," she muttered under her breath. "I'm Gail. I'm Mhirran's friend." Her eyes closed in concentration. A smile wobbled at the side of her mouth. She was doing it. She'd remembered herself. Kay would be so—

Gail choked, her eyes shocked open. Panic bubbled in her throat. Kay. She'd lost her shadow *again*. What would Francis do with it? A sickness rose in her stomach and she leaned forward to stop her head from spinning. When she looked up, the bird's shadow was still at her feet and Jake's eyes were wide with worry.

"What's wrong with it?" she burst out, the pufferfish prickling inside her. And then, quieter: "What's wrong with me?"

Gail didn't think he could have heard her. But he did. He cleared his throat awkwardly and a wind whipped through his curls.

"Maybe you've forgotten where your edges are," Jake said carefully. "Forgotten what shape you make." He shrugged. "If you've lost your shape, you can't make a shadow."

Gail snorted and threw another branch into the flames angrily, but Jake's words swam inside her and she heard an echo of Mhirran's voice. *You've lost yourself, Gail. You can't cast a shadow if you're not really here.*

"It's okay," Jake said simply, his hand hovering at her shoulder. "You'll get it back."

Gail shrugged his hand away. "Nothing's okay. Francis has got Kay's shadow, and I can't get rid of this stupid bird and he could do anything—" Her voice broke and she jabbed at the fire. "He's a monster."

Grey smudges slipped across Jake's face. In the strained silence, Gail could hear the wind rising to a howl, rattling the tree canopy above.

Finally, Jake asked, "Do you think I'm a monster?"

Gail frowned and shook her head. "You're helping me," she said firmly. Though even as she said it, she felt the bird's shadow squirm at her feet, stronger, but still firmly attached. *Was* he helping her? And would the owners of the shadows which quivered in his pockets have called him a monster? Gail bit her lip. But if he couldn't help it...

Jake read the uncertainty in her eyes and nodded. "'Monster' is a big word, Gail. And what you name people matters."

Gail squirmed as she felt the edges of her own name in her mouth. *Gale.*

When Jake next spoke, his voice had dropped to the

crackle of the fire's embers. "Did Mhirran ever tell you about her parents?"

A squirrel leapt between two trees high above them. Gail shook her head.

"They died. They were both killed in a storm last year." Jake caught her expression. "No, it wasn't me. Lightning struck a huge oak and..." Jake shifted and his pockets twitched and turned. "Mhirran didn't speak for five months afterwards. Not a word. Her uncle took her out of school. He tried everything to make her speak, but nothing worked. And then, one day, he started talking to her about talking. You know, about all the different ways creatures speak to each other: birds, wolves, crickets... After a while, she got curious. She started reading more about it. The first thing she said, after those five months, was that elephants can sense the warning calls of other elephants through the ground. They feel it with their feet."

Jake smiled at the memory. "That was the first time I met her. She was so astonished by it. Her eyes were all lit up. She didn't care about the wind that kept tangling her hair whenever she sat by me, or about the shadows in my pockets, she just wanted me to say something really loud while she'd stick her fingers in her ears and try to hear it through her feet.

"We became friends after that, and she told me

about all these ways of talking, and of the codes she'd learned." Jake frowned. "She said that Francis thought that it was just another kind of silence, this talking in codes. But it isn't."

Gail's mouth fell open. Of course. All of Mhirran's constant chatter was about talking. She hadn't listened hard enough. Bird calls and Morse code, dolphin clicks, spiderweb vibrations and whistling languages. Gail bit her lip. And she'd dismissed Mhirran's words just like Francis had: *You talk all the time, but you don't ever say anything real.*

Jake glanced at the bird by Gail's feet and continued. "It affected Francis differently. After their parents died, he got really quiet too, but in a different way. He didn't believe they were gone. Couldn't believe it. So, when he found out about the storms and the shadows that stuck to storms, he began searching. He was sure he could find his parents' shadows."

The embers of the fire crackled suddenly and Gail spun round, half-expecting to see Francis leaning over her. "So that's who he meant," she said. "He said he was looking for two shadows. But he's not found them."

"He's still looking. Maybe one day…"

"But the birds, what has he done to them? And why does he want my sister's shadow?" She flicked her fringe out of her eyes angrily. "He knew she was my sister and he just—" Gail's mind filled with the vampire squid shape of Francis's shadow-swallowing machine.

Jake chewed his lip and the wind tunnelled around him, sending currents which licked at Gail's face. "What he's doing to those shadows isn't right. But..." His face creased into a frown. Slowly, as if he was trying to figure it out himself, he began. "Storms are violent, Gail. We batter and hurl and flood and burn. We are the release of so much anger and energy." Jake scratched his head. "And it's like... since that night, a storm began to grow inside Francis's heart, and it's just kept on growing." Jake shook his head. "But there's nowhere for it to go, so it's just twisting away inside him.

"He became obsessed with the hunt for these shadows, staying out all night, not eating..." Jake shrugged. "And the more time he spent with shadows, the more he became lost in his own world. He started experimenting on them, trying to 'fix' them, so that he'd know what to do when he found his parents."

"He thought he could bring them back?" Gail breathed.

Jake nodded. "I think so. That storm petrel picture on the shed door: his mum painted it. Both his dad and mum loved birds. It's why they were in the forest that night the lightning hit the tree: they were bird-watching. What he did to these bird shadows," Jake gestured to Gail's feet, "it's like he's trying to please his parents by giving back flight to something they loved. And it's practice for when he finds them."

"And me? He wanted me and Kay's shadow to help find his parents' shadows, didn't he?" Francis's words spun through Gail's mind. *Blood ties and family bonds. It's the next step.* "What was he going to do to us?"

Jake chewed on his lip. "I don't know. Maybe he doesn't even know."

Gail stared at the bird's shadow preening its feathers at her feet. "And Mhirran... She's..." The argument outside the caves caught at Gail's throat. She had accused Mhirran of helping him. *Francis is my brother, Gail.* "She's not helping him, is she?"

Jake smiled sadly. "Mhirran?" He shook his head. "She follows him and stays with him and sees what he's doing and hates it. She doesn't know what else to do. She slows him down in small ways. Damages his machines, misses shadows when she's meant to be catching them."

A laugh burst out of Gail and surprised them both. "I just thought she was clumsy," she explained, recalling Mhirran treading on the machine as they moved through the tunnels, and Francis's anger at her missing Kay's shadow as it slipped through the cavern.

Jake frowned. "But he's her brother. He's all she's got left, now. Along with her uncle."

Gail smiled as hair the colour of sunrise appeared from between the trees.

"And us," she said.

Chapter Nineteen

When Mhirran saw Gail, her face lit up then immediately crumpled and words tumbled out of her mouth. "I'm sorry Gail last night I couldn't stop him I tried but he heard you and today the birds I never thought the shadow would drop you and I wanted to come straight here but I had to follow him and I hid and I let them out. I opened it up Gail and I let them out but Kay's shadow was so quick and he was coming I had to be fast and she's gone and I'm sorry."

She collapsed by the fire, her glasses sliding hopelessly down her nose. Jake pushed them gently back up.

"You let Kay's shadow out?"

Mhirran nodded miserably.

"She's free?"

Her hair swung up and down.

Gail catapulted towards her, the shadow flapping at her feet, shocking her into a hug. "You got her out of the chest!"

Gail squeezed Mhirran as tight as she could, but when she let go, the smile on Mhirran's face didn't quite reach her eyes. She turned to Jake.

"He knows," she said in the smallest voice Gail had ever heard. "He knows I let them go."

A soft wind ruffled her hair as Jake squeezed her arm. "You did the right thing," he said.

Mhirran looked at Gail helplessly. "I'm sorry, Gail. I should have stopped him sooner. What he did to you, to those bird shadows. It's just..." Her voice trailed away as she stared at the crumple of feathers still clinging to Gail's feet.

Gail took a deep breath. "He's your brother, Mhirran," she finished for her.

Mhirran nodded, her eyes bright as a blue tang as they met Gail's. "I knew you'd understand," she said. Then her mouth twitched and she let out a familiar piercing call. *Krrrrrrhuh Krrrrrrrhuh.*

It felt for a second like everything in the forest was holding its breath. Then, in a scrumple of dark feathers, another petrel shadow landed next to Gail.

"It's the other bird shadow?" Gail asked, wide-eyed. "Why?"

The second petrel reached tentatively towards the shadow fluttering at Gail's foot.

"Look. Maybe this is the answer to your problem, Gail," Jake murmured.

The shadow at Gail's feet recognised its companion, sending tingles through her body. She could feel its impatient excitement. "What's happening?"

"Watch," Jake whispered, and so Gail did. She watched the shadow at her feet fluff up its oil-black feathers and open its wings. She watched the second dark blur trill a silent call to the first, and she watched as, slowly, the first shadow dropped away from her shoes, smudging into the second in a spinning dance of darkness. Then, in a spiral of twisting grey, both shadows stretched out their wings and lifted together into the sky.

Gail wriggled her toes in relief, staring at the birds as they became specks above the creaking trees. "But... I don't understand."

Jake smiled. "There are ties between shadows as well, Gail. Stronger ties than we could guess at."

Once the bird shadows were out of sight, Gail tucked her feet beneath her, holding her own edges close to herself.

"When Kay's shadow escaped the chest," Mhirran said, drawing closer to the fire, "it moved so fast, as if it knew exactly where it was going. It moved like ink, like it was swimming over the ground. And it was heading south, Gail. Why?"

Gail stopped to think. Mhirran was right. Even when she had first chased Kay's shadow away, it felt like it knew exactly where it was going. Like it was trying to get somewhere.

"I don't know." It hurt that she didn't. She should know. Kay was her sister.

"If Kay's shadow is heading south," Mhirran said, thinking aloud, "then it's going in the same direction as Femi and the other boys. If we follow the map he left, then we'll be following Kay's shadow too."

Gail winced. She'd felt in her pockets for the map when she'd dried off from the loch, but it had gone. "I lost the map, Mhirran. I don't think we'll find him without it." She squeezed the pearl tight in her fist and it bit into her palm.

Mhirran grinned and pulled the thin sheet of paper out of her coat. "You gave it to me, remember?" she said. "When we were walking to the waterfall." She turned to Jake. "Do you recognise this tree?" she asked, frowning at the pine with the jagged branch.

He stole a look and nodded. "You can't miss it. It's on its own, metres from where the woods end. From there, you'll see this path which'll take you along the ridge over the swamp, down to the bothy and towards the ravine where the river is. Unusual, that." He tapped the cross on the map. "Choosing a river deep in a ravine." He glanced at Mhirran's wrist, now wrapped in a tight bandage. "It's quite a way, and it's a scramble in places. You'll have to go slow."

Mhirran nodded. "I'm okay."

Jake blinked and looked upwards at the dark clouds. "You'll get wet."

"What's this?" Gail asked suddenly. She pointed to two circles drawn on the edge of the cliff, close to the island's southern tip.

"Eilidh and Mor," Jake replied, with a strange shine in his eye. "Though not many people know them by those names. Around here, they're called the Storm Sisters."

Gail's eyes widened. "The Storm Sisters? The giants?"

Jake nodded. "There's a place where you can go—"

"To be sheltered inside a storm," Gail finished.

"A hollow cave, between the two sisters. I've been there before," Jake said.

Gail's heart beat against her ribs as she stared at them. "*This* is where Kay's shadow is going," she said. "I know it! We were going to go there together, at the next storm. This is where it's been headed all along!"

She bit her lip in excitement and drew her finger over the map from Femi's cross at the river mouth to the two rocks at the edge of the island. There was only a short distance between them. "We'll stop Femi and then find Kay's shadow," she announced, and as she stood, she saw a rustle behind a birch tree. She stepped closer, holding her breath.

Two eyes, not three metres from where she stood, blinked slowly at her. Eyes like coral glow, like a broken sunset. Gail grinned. A flicker ran through her body, like a breeze was spinning inside her. "Hello again," she whispered to the cat as it crouched in the undergrowth, its ears flat against its head.

She heard the others shift behind her.

For one moment, the cat watched her, then it twitched its nose and turned, disappearing into the forest.

"Isn't it beautiful?" she breathed as she turned around.

She was not prepared for the look on Mhirran and Jake's faces. Their eyes were moon-pale and alive with astonishment.

"But—" Mhirran began. "That's a *wildcat*. We just saw a wildcat," she spluttered.

"A wildcat?"

Mhirran's eyes gleamed. "Gail, they're really really rare. Endangered. I've never seen one around here. No one's seen one."

"I saw it before. After the deer herd ran through

the woods," Gail said. Then she frowned. "What is it, Jake?"

Shadows wound themselves in spirals around Jake's ears. He tapped the map, close to the edge of the woods. "Someone's drawn a wildcat on this rock in chalk. I saw it early this morning. Maybe it was this Femi you keep talking about," he said.

Gail remembered the drawing she'd seen from high above the loch. It must have been the wildcat. "But why—?" she began.

Then she stopped. She spun back to where the real cat had been. She tapped her teeth and began to pace. Pacing was what Kay did when she was thinking she should be thinking. Gail knew she was missing something, some connection. She walked up and down, turning the pearl around and around inside her pocket as Jake and Mhirran watched her. The pearl that Femi had left her. The freshwater mussels. The manta ray. The drawing of the hawksbill turtle in Kay's room. Why would he leave a drawing of a wildcat? Why would he mark his way? Gail stopped and spun round to Mhirran.

"You said it's endangered? The wildcat?"

Mhirran nodded and Gail's eyes widened suddenly in realisation.

"They all are," she breathed. "They're all endangered.

Everything he draws. He isn't *hunting* pearls. He'll know they're endangered too. He's trying to save them!" Gail scrunched her forehead together. "Remember, Mhirran. What did you say he drew? A sea lion, a reef of coral..."

"A sea turtle." Mhirran stared. "The manta ray. Are they all endangered?"

Gail nodded. "Or vulnerable. Just like the freshwater mussels."

Mhirran opened her mouth and closed it again.

"That's why he left Kay the map," Gail rushed on. "She must have said she'd help him. Before she started sinking," she added, under her breath.

Mhirran smiled. "I knew it," she said. "I knew it! Femi wouldn't join pearl thieves."

Gail pulled the mussel shell out of her pocket. "But what's his plan?" she asked. "Why would he lead pearl fishers to that part of the island?"

"He's told you." Jake smiled. He was holding Femi's paper map up against the darkening sky. Mhirran and Gail jostled at his elbows, their hair knotting in the wind that wrapped around him. "Look."

There, in tiny letters surrounding the cross, as if it were a compass, Femi had written:

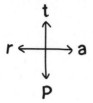

Gail stared. "A trap? He's planning to trap them?"

Mhirran scrunched up her nose. "That sounds dangerous."

"And difficult," Jake said.

"And stupid," added Gail, and she caught Mhirran's eye and grinned. "Alright," she said. "Let's go save Femi, trap the pearl fishers and find my sister's shadow," and her eyes flashed as the wind spun inside her hair.

Chapter Twenty

Trees creaked and groaned like the bones of an old ship as grey clouds rolled towards them. The sky was ragged and heavy with rain. Gail glanced back at Mhirran striding behind her, relieved to have her company on the long walk. Jake hadn't come with them. Mhirran had said it was because of the storm coming. "He's scared of them," she'd said.

Gail had laughed. "You're kidding?"

And Mhirran had grinned back. "I know, right?" Now she looked up at Gail and nudged her glasses further up her nose thoughtfully. "You seem different, Gail. More solid or something." She paused. "Did you see your shadow again?"

Gail pulled a face and shook her head. Mhirran was right: she did feel more solid, less blurry around the edges. But the space beneath her feet was still empty.

Looking up, she stopped walking and stared. Was she imagining it? She rubbed her eyes. It was still there. A dark patch, small but distinct despite the thunderclouds, was flowing over the grass on a low hill further ahead. Gail's heart pounded. Even from this distance, she knew it wasn't hers. It was unmistakably Kay's shadow, free of Francis and rushing south, just as Mhirran had described.

"Look!" She lurched forward, pointing. "Do you see it, Mhirran?" Gail asked, hope soaring through her as the shadow dipped from sight into a valley. "Did you see Kay's shadow?"

Mhirran beamed at her. "It's going the same way we're going. And see over there, too. We've found Femi's drawing."

Gail followed Mhirran's finger until she saw the bright chalk markings she'd first glimpsed from the sky.

Where the trees thinned, a rock balanced oddly, as if on tiptoe, at the edge of the woods. They drew closer and saw clearly the white wildcat shape. The cat's tail was lifted like a calligraphic flourish behind it, and its stomach was low, as if on the prowl. Looking for something.

"What do you think Femi's planning?" Mhirran asked as they stared at the rock. "How's he going to trap them?"

Gail chewed her lip. "I'm not sure," she said. "But

he must have something in mind." The not-knowing gnawed at her. "I wish we knew how Kay was going to help him... He needs us to do something, I think. Something he can't do by himself. What could it be?"

Mhirran pulled the map from her pocket, flattening it against the ear of the chalk wildcat, and looked between the pictures and their surroundings.

"There—" She pointed to their right. "That must be the tree."

Gail squinted at a tall pine, solitary and stern on a steep hill further south, and nodded, but before they could walk on, a shriek of birds exploded from the forest a little way behind them.

Mhirran spun around. "Someone's following us."

Gail scrambled up onto the rock. From the top, she could see a lean figure, a long way behind them, moving between the trees. He was striding quickly, with something heavy pulling at his back.

"It's Francis." Gail slid down, her face as hard as the stone she stood next to. "He's coming after Kay's shadow, isn't he?"

Mhirran didn't need to answer. Gail squeezed her hand, took the map and folded it carefully into her pocket. "Let's go," she said. "From the tree, we should be able to find the way." One branch of the swaying pine reached out like a hand to the west, its wooden fingers pointing to the faintest trace of a path, raised high along the rocky ridge.

The island was narrowing and their eyes were filled with the sea, whale-grey with toothpaste smears of white where the wind chewed at the water. The land rose and fell like waves, jagged at the edges, and everything stood waiting beneath the rising storm. A lochan beneath them blinked like an eye as clouds rolled across it, watching their movements as they inched closer to the far point of the island.

"Jake said we should stay on the high path." Gail struggled to make herself heard over the wind that tore through her hair. "Francis won't know about the swamp. He might try and cut through the valley and by the lochan towards the bothy." She pointed to a low stone hut in the distance. "The swamp will slow him down."

She turned back to her friend. Her words were muffled by the hair flung inside her mouth, but Mhirran understood the hand that reached out to her. They gazed ahead towards the rocky southern point of the island. Kay's shadow must be somewhere among those sharp points and drops. Inch by inch, and hand in hand, the two girls made their way along the ridge.

When the path finally dipped down, they hurried past the bothy, its dark windows cobwebbed and watchful. Francis was nowhere to be seen. Boulders grew around them and, as the rocky finger of island narrowed, they heard the distinct ripple of moving water.

"We're close to the ravine," Gail whispered, as Mhirran bumped against her shoulder. "Stay down in case Femi and those boys are nearby."

Jake had explained that a river tumbled out of the southern end of the island, just this side of the Storm Sisters. Near where it reached the sea, the river had carved a deep fissure into the rocks. He'd said they might be able to get down into it on this side if they followed the path from behind the bothy.

They inched forward, slipping between rocks and thorny gorse bushes, keeping their heads hidden. Every now and then, Gail stuck her face out to scan ahead.

At last she glimpsed the wet shine of water down on their right: it was the river running below a cliff face on its far side that reared up two metres tall, the rock sheer and smooth as an eel. Her eyes searched for Femi.

"No sign," she hissed. Another dash between rocks.

"Nothing." Another sprint. Another skipped heartbeat.

Then they heard a rough shuffling ahead. Feet on rocks. Gail hesitated for a second, unease prickling within her. She inched cautiously closer. As they began to curve around a rock face, they heard the sudden rise of a voice, then a sharp grunt of pain. Gail turned back to Mhirran, and saw her own fear reflected in Mhirran's wide eyes. They pressed themselves back against the rock, its slope hiding them from sight.

"I knew you were up to something! You're leaving marks so someone will find us. Aren't you, Femi?"

Gail peered past the rock. Femi was metres from them, his face pressed against a boulder and his arm twisted sharply behind his back. Euan had him pinned. Gail could see the bruising of his fingers around Femi's wrist. The other boy hovered close by, a piece of chalk crushed beneath his boot.

"Who's this for?" Euan jerked his head towards a scrap of white drawing on the rock behind Femi. It looked almost like a flipper.

Femi winced. "I wasn't—"

"I told you, Euan." The other boy's face was tight with worry. "It's a trick. He's leading someone to us. Let's get out of here."

Euan turned to him and growled, "Shut up, Gus.

Look at him. We're not running from him. If he's lied to us, I'm sure his dad won't be pleased to find out we caught him pearl fishing in the river – again," he sneered.

Gail swallowed hard. Femi's head twisted, and his eyes were dark like wet stones in his face. Then he saw her and a strangled noise grew from his throat. Gail thrust herself back behind the rock, holding her breath.

"What's that?" Gus asked abruptly. Gail heard him walk closer. "He saw something," Gus said to Euan.

"I-I- wasn't leading anyone anywhere," she heard Femi stutter out, and the footsteps slowed. "Except you. I said I'd show you where you'd find them – the oldest, biggest mussels – and I have. They're just up there."

"Take us then," Euan snarled, releasing Femi and pushing him towards the ravine. Femi stumbled forward with the other two close at his heels. Gail watched them move upriver, clambering around stony outcrops along the top of the ravine wall, until they were out of sight.

Behind the rock, Mhirran's hands were flapping in panic. "What now?" she whispered.

Gail caught Mhirran's hands to still them and tried to make her thoughts go faster, but all she could see was the dark wet panic in Femi's eyes. *What now what now what now.* What did Femi need from them? How could they help him? What would Kay have done? She took a deep breath, chewing furiously at her lips, but her thoughts were scattered and confused. It felt like trying to do maths homework, all the numbers swimming around the page.

Gail breathed out. That was it. *When the numbers swim, swim with them,* Kay always said when Gail got stuck. Then she'd pick up the page and spin it around three times. She'd tell Gail to stand up, close her eyes and push her arms through the air in breaststroke, and then she'd put the sum in front of her again saying, *Go back to the beginning. Go right back to the very beginning and start again.*

"Um. What are you doing, Gail?"

Moving your arms through the air like breaststroke while crouched in a ball behind a rock was surprisingly awkward. "We've got to go back to the beginning, Mhirran."

"Back to the beginning?" Mhirran repeated.

Gail nodded and opened her eyes. "So, first: he left a map for Kay."

"And Kay must have known he'd leave it," Mhirran continued. "They must have had a plan. Then once he knew she wasn't coming he told you he needed something, but we don't know what."

Gail frowned. "He drew me another map on the ground. And he drew us signs. The manta ray, and the wildcat, and this turtle fin."

"He used the pictures to show us the way, like a code."

Gail's voice glittered with excitement. "But he must have always known where he was going – right from the start, when he drew the first map. He wanted to bring them *here*."

"Right," Mhirran said, her eyes glowing. "And if he knows they're endangered creatures, he wouldn't lead Euan to a real mussel river, would he?"

Gail nodded furiously. "He's brought them here because this place is—"

"This *is* the trap," Mhirran finished. They grinned at each other.

"So I think I know what he needs. It's like Jake warned us. Someone could probably get down into the ravine by themselves, but they wouldn't be able to get back out without help." Gail straightened. "You've got to get me down there, Mhirran," she said.

Chapter Twenty-one

By the time her toes scraped the ground, Gail was convinced her arm had stretched by at least ten centimetres. Mhirran was holding Gail's hand with her good wrist, lowering her down the side of the ravine. The skin was grazed off both Gail's knees and her shoulder ached from the strain, but when she landed with a clap of bruised bones and scattered stones, she patted off the worst of the damage and grinned up at her friend.

"Made it," she whispered.

The ledge Mhirran knelt on was a short clamber down from the full height of the ravine wall. It hadn't taken them long to find it, following Jake's description. Mhirran held Gail's rucksack close, and when Gail raised her eyebrows, she nodded firmly, though her chin quivered.

"We can do this," Gail said quietly, as she edged backwards towards the river, the wind whipping around her cheeks, stinging her ears and drawing the storm closer.

Mhirran tapped a sequence of dots and scrapes on the rock beneath her. "Good luck," she mouthed. And then she disappeared.

Gail took a deep breath and turned to the river. This had to work. The water hurtled towards the coastal cliff edge, where she could just see the spray as it fell down towards the ocean. Another waterfall. She smiled to herself.

As she rounded a bend of the river, her breath stuck in her throat. They were huge. Two giants of stone, their heads leaning in to each other. The Storm Sisters, sitting right at the edge of the sea cliff. They were so beautiful she stopped suddenly, one hand half-raised in the air towards them, as if in greeting.

"HEY!"

Gail spun around. Euan loomed at the edge of the ravine. "What are you up to?"

Gail swallowed hard. She could do this. She shrugged one shoulder in a way she hoped looked half-guilty, half-defensive. It was a lot to ask of a shoulder shrug. "N-nothing," she stammered. She stepped backwards and carefully let the mussel shell drop from her pocket, as if by accident.

"What's that?" Euan's voice was sharp with accusation.

Gail hurried to pick up the shell. "It's nothing, just a mussel," she mumbled. She waved it in the air for him to see, her smile wobbling.

"It's big," Euan said slowly. "Really big."

Gail paused. She was a terrible liar, Kay always said so. "Is it?" she asked tentatively.

Euan turned and shouted something over his shoulder and Gus appeared at the edge of the ravine. Gail's throat constricted. Where was Femi?

Gus nodded towards Gail. "Looks like a freshwater mussel you have there," he said, cautiously. He lowered his voice and turned to Euan, but Gail still caught his next words: "Femi was right."

"Seen any more of them around here?" Euan asked. His question was heavy with forced lightness.

Gail bit her lip. "Are you looking for them?"

Euan and Gus exchanged glances. They nodded and Gail smiled innocently. "There's loads," she said, gesturing at the river behind her. "And look." In her hand she held up the small pearl Femi had left. She heard Euan's sharp intake of breath and Gus's urgent muttering, his head close to Euan's.

"How did you get down there?" Gus shouted out at last.

Gail pointed back round the bend of the river towards the ledge. "It's less steep there," she directed, and they nodded, striding away, their faces tight with expectation.

Hearing their muffled curses as they slipped and scrambled down the rock face, Gail tried to bite back the grin that bloomed on her face. The plan was working.

She looked up at a noise and saw Femi approaching the edge of the ravine, just above where she was standing. Spotting her, his eyes widened.

"What are you doing?" he hissed.

"We're helping you," Gail whispered up to him.

"We?" Femi asked, then shrank back when Gus and Euan rounded the corner.

Gail threw the shell high in the air and Euan snatched it as it fell, pulling it close to his eyes. A look of greed crawled across his face. "Show us the pearl, then," he said, while Gus removed a bucket from his pack, rolled up his trousers and waded into the water.

Gail's palm closed around the pearl and she could feel its smoothness press against her skin. She glanced up to where she was sure Femi must be crouched, watching, but he wasn't there. Her eyes scanned the edge of the ravine, raking over rocks and gorse. Where had he gone? And where was Mhirran? She should be here by now.

Euan tapped the shell against his teeth as Gail reluctantly held out the pearl. When he reached for it, she pulled back.

"Find your own," she said, her light words betrayed by the ripple of unease running through them. "You've seen pearls before," she added, but Euan's eyes glittered, and she realised he hadn't. He'd never found one.

She moved away and turned so she was backing along the riverbed. Euan was between her and the ravine wall where she'd seen Femi. She glanced behind his shoulders but there was no one above.

Euan half-stepped forward, then turned to follow her gaze. "What are you looking at?" he asked, and Gail could hear suspicion stinging his voice. His eyes narrowed and he stared at the mussel shell in his hand then back at Gail. "Why did you say you were here?" he growled. "How do you know about this place? Who told you?"

Gail stumbled backwards and opened her mouth to reply when Gus shouted out behind them, "Euan, there's nothing here. Look." Shooting a warning glare at Gail, Euan strode over to where Gus crouched with his hands deep in the water. "There're no mussels at all."

Both boys stared at Gail. Euan's eyes flashed dangerously and Gus's lean body quivered with tension.

Gail could feel her heart beating like a fish's tail

against her ribs, pounding at her chest. "But-but-I found it," she stammered out. "I did... Right here."

They straightened, fists tightening at their sides, and panic rose inside her. It had all gone wrong. They knew she'd lied to them and now there was no way out. She was trapped, and could only stumble backwards as Euan and Gus stalked towards her. A deep growl of thunder sounded in the distance.

Then, out the corner of her eye, she saw a flicker of something orange at the edge of the rocky ravine wall above.

"Gail!" a small clear voice cried out.

And she ran. She ran towards the arms that reached out to her, leaning down over the cliff edge. She yelped as Euan darted after her and clutched at her coat, and tore herself away from him, leaping onto a stone to throw herself upwards, her hands open and trusting in the loose air until she found Femi and Mhirran, who each grasped one hand tightly. They pulled her up, her feet and knees scrambling and grazing once again on the smooth rock, until she lay panting on the ground, high above the river, her head in Mhirran's lap and her foot tangled beneath Femi's shoe.

"You're stronger than you look," she said at last, catching her breath, and Mhirran grinned at her. "So are you," she said.

Femi was on his feet, leaning out over the edge of the ravine wall. He had his phone in his hand and he took photo after photo of Euan holding the mussel shell and Gus with his bucket, scratching and swearing at the smooth wall of rock.

Throwing the shell aside, Euan stormed towards the ledge they'd used to get down, but Femi shouted after him: "You're trapped, Euan. It's too high to climb back up. And even if you could, we've barred the way with gorse. Unless you want to get cut to pieces, you'll have to walk the long way back along the river."

Euan's fists clutched at the empty air. "No one will believe you, Femi."

Femi shrugged. The graze on his cheek stood out starkly and his eyes were dark like the deep sea, but his voice was quiet, almost gentle. "No one has to. I've got photos. And it's not just me they'll be believing."

Gail and Mhirran rose up beside him and the three of them stared down at the boys.

"I gave you so many chances to turn back," Femi said. "You knew that you'd be killing them. And that they're endangered."

From up here, they looked so much younger, Gail thought. Gus's face was pale with guilt.

"We won't do it again," he babbled. "We promise.

We won't, will we, Euan?" He lurched forwards. "It wasn't my idea. Don't tell anyone, Femi, please."

Femi looked at Gail and she raised her eyebrows, turning to Euan. "Well?"

Euan pushed Gus to one side and glowered up at them. His eyes were flat and furious as they met Gail's. But she held his gaze with the steady intensity of the wildcat and, as the wind roared around them and the ocean spat and churned beyond the cliff, Euan nodded. Just once. Then he turned and, without a word, began the long walk up the ravine river. Gus hastened after him and Gail breathed out.

Femi squeezed Gail's shoulder. "Thanks, wildcat." He grinned.

"It was both of us," Gail said, as Mhirran handed back the rucksack and placed a gentle hand on Gail's arm.

Mhirann nodded towards the cliffs. "We're almost there," she murmured.

Gail looked to the Storm Sisters and hope rose inside her. She was so close to Kay's shadow. She faced her friends. "Can I go first, for this next bit? It's just—" She shrugged.

Mhirran nodded. "We'll be right behind you," she said, as the first heavy drops of rain splashed onto Gail's cheeks.

Chapter Twenty-two

The two Storm Sisters rose like waves at the edge of the cliff. Gail could see the arch of their backs amongst the ripple and gnarl of the stone. She could make out the bracing of their shoulders and, as the river fell to the right of them and she drew closer, the wide face of the smaller Sister, looking out to sea. She had to squint at first, but when she saw it, she couldn't stop seeing it. A broad slab of a nose and the faintest ripple of rock that could be the tremor of a mouth.

CRACK!

The storm broke; thunder split the sky. Rain fell hard and fast, thick driving sheets of it that soaked through Gail's coat and stung her cheeks. She felt each clap of thunder vibrate deep inside her ribs while the wind howled around her, chewing at her hair and freezing her fingertips. She fought against it, stumbling onward along the ravine edge. When she looked back over her shoulder, she could no longer see her friends.

Nearing the Sisters, Gail slowed. There was a pull here, something magnetic. *The rock must be so old, millions of years old*, she thought. *Older than everything.* The Sisters stood at the lip of the river, where the water surged forward towards the cliff edge. Gail hesitated, pushing her wet fringe from her eyes. She knew she should be hurrying to find Kay's shadow. But now, at the end of her journey, she was afraid. What if it kept running from her? What if it didn't want to be found?

As Gail stepped slowly closer, she glimpsed the sheltered opening between the Sisters, above a rocky ledge. She reached out a hand to touch the stone and shivered as something rippled through her. Something deep and ancient, like what she'd felt back home when she and Kay had dipped their toes in the carpet-ocean.

The opening was at the height of her nose, and Gail scrambled up onto the ledge awkwardly, her legs splayed, reaching for jaggy footholds and clutching at the rock, slippery with rain. The wind roared around her like a wild animal, whipping her hair into a frenzy. Then at last she was inside, shuffling forwards into the still gloom as the storm pounded above her.

It smelled blue and sharp and salty. And it was quiet. The storm and the ocean were nothing but murmurs from inside the small cave. Like wingbeats, back and forth. The space was less than two metres deep, and not high enough to stand in. Gail crawled to the back and turned around. Through the cave opening, she could see more thunderclouds darkening like bruises in the sky. Here she was, held between two Sisters in the middle of a storm. Just like Kay had wanted. Just where they would have come, together, for this first storm after summer.

But Kay wasn't with her. Kay was at home, alone, sinking. And as Gail stared around the cave, she realised that she, too, was completely alone: Kay's shadow wasn't at the Storm Sisters.

Gail was sure that this was where the shadow had been heading. Nothing else made sense. And it had been far ahead of them when they'd seen the wildcat drawing: it would have arrived at the Sisters before her. But it must have moved on. In the midst of the raging storm, and despite the shelter here. She had no idea where or why it had gone.

Gail collapsed against the cold stone wall. It felt like she was made of sand. Like a wave had reached out to lick her heart, and her whole body had come tumbling down. She'd failed. She'd promised Kay that she'd bring her shadow back, but she'd lost it.

A sound outside. A flicker of movement caught

Gail's eye, and her breath stopped. There was no mistaking the thin figure heading towards the Sisters. Francis had found her.

She put her hand flat against the old stone and tried to slow her breathing. She couldn't face him now. Not without Kay's shadow. Not when everything had gone so wrong. Perhaps he wouldn't look in here. If she could just stay hidden...

Retreating, she curled her head into her body and noticed something stuck down the side of her boot. She reached to tug it free, and her hands trembled as she pulled out a scrap of the manta ray poster she'd ripped up yesterday in Kay's room. It felt like so long ago. The memory ached inside her. But as her breath fluttered the damp piece of paper, she glimpsed something scrawled on the back. A dark scribble, the ink half-blurred. Gail squinted. It was Kay's handwriting, and it read:

For Gale. Happy Birt

For Gale. For Gale. Gail lifted it to her eyes, so that the name filled them. Kay had called her *Gale*. Inside her ribs, her heart leapt, over and over, like a manta ray jumping out of the ocean.

When Gail straightened, everything was alight: her bones, her eyes, her fingertips. She wasn't going to hide any more. For a second her legs hung uncertainly off the ledge at the opening, and then she jumped forward into the storm, landing right in front of Francis. Her eyes blazed and it was as if a thread of wind split from the sky to spin around her, unfurling her hair into a sea anemone. Francis stepped backwards.

"Gail," he sneered, recovering himself. "What a pleasure."

Anger bloomed in Gail's body, the pufferfish spiking her stomach. He had taken Kay's shadow from her. He had thrown her into the sky with bird shadows at her feet and her arms. He had hunted her through the forest. She saw the thick wood of the shadow swallower at his shoulder and hated him for it. She knew Kay's shadow wasn't in there. She could feel it was empty.

When she moved, she moved so fast that Francis didn't have time to react. She moved like a gale was inside her, pulling the wooden chest from his back and heaving it up in her arms even as her shoulders burned with the effort. She lifted it high above her head and threw it down into the ravine, where it tumbled, crashing into the water, and was sucked instantly towards the waterfall.

It was over so suddenly.

One hand still clutching at her jumper from

his attempt to stop her, Francis stood beside Gail, watching as the river took his shadow swallower over the sea cliff to splinter and tear on the rocks below and sink beneath the ocean. Rain poured down his cheeks.

When he spoke, Gail shrank from the ice-white agony of his voice. "What have you done? How could you—"

His eyes were wide, and, for the first time, Gail saw the storm within him that Jake had described. Flashes of pain and the thunder of a loss he couldn't face. And Gail knew then that there were moments her own eyes looked like that. Storm-eyes. Helpless and full of anger. She swallowed.

"You took my sister's shadow from me. How could you do that?" Her voice strained. "You have a sister, Francis." Gail stared at the river surging over the sea cliff and struggled to put everything into words. It was all too big for her head.

Francis's loss spooled out of him like ink. Gail closed her eyes, and she saw again the storm roiling inside him. She saw the loneliness that yawned at his centre, and it shocked her out of her confusion.

No one should be alone.

"You have a sister, Francis," she repeated. "You're not alone."

Francis ignored her. "It. Was. Everything. To me.

Everything I had worked for. How could you?"

Gail's voice rose and she turned to face him. "But you're not alone, Francis. You've got Mhirran. Talk to Mhirran!"

Francis shrugged her away, his eyes hooded. "Ha! My sister only talks in riddles."

Gail scowled. "Then work them out."

Krrrrrrhuh Krrrrrrrhuh. Gail spun around. Mhirran walked slowly towards them. On each shoulder, a petrel shadow sat, nibbling at her wet hair. Francis stared at the shadows and Mhirran stared at Francis.

"Whatever bad things you've done to them, they're beautiful," she whispered. She nodded slightly to her right shoulder, her hair brushing across the shadow. "I've called this one Feather," she said. Francis grimaced and turned away, back towards the river and the thrash of water over the edge. Mhirran moved closer and Gail saw her mouth tighten as she struggled with something too big for one person to struggle with alone.

When Mhirran next spoke, Gail knew she was pulling the words up from a deep, secret part of herself. "I named her after Mum," she said at last, to Francis's turned back. "Because she always had so many feathers in her pockets. Do you remember? Do you remember that time we turned her coat pockets out and counted them?" Mhirran's eyes were soft, like light through sea glass. The rain wrinkled through her hair and dripped steadily off her nose.

She looked from Gail to Francis, and one of the petrels leaned against her ear, its swirling darkness a slow whirlwind by her face.

"It's okay, Gail," Mhirran said. "Go and find Femi." She looked back at the Sisters and at Gail's empty feet. "He's seen what you're looking for."

As Gail hurried away, she heard Mhirran's gentle voice behind her: "I thought you could name this one, Francis."

Chapter Twenty-three

Not far from the Storm Sisters, Femi was sketching the carapace of a Kemp's ridley sea turtle, even as the rain washed the chalk away. Gail arrived breathlessly behind him.

"You saw it? Mhirran said you saw it?" Gail's heart flapped in her throat when Femi nodded.

His eyes brushed her feet. "You never said yours had gone too."

Gail scanned the ground around her. "Where did you see it, Femi? It wasn't at the Sisters. Where did it go?"

Femi gestured towards a narrow path winding between rocks and through patches of heather, right to the edge of the high sea cliff. Gail peered past him. The path edged in a slow zigzag down the side of the cliff, dropping at last into a cove, the beach sandy and distant. She swayed and caught her breath.

"Straight down here." Femi turned back to Gail and

grinned, mischief dancing in his eyes. "I knew it was yours as soon as I saw it. It had the same prickle about it. The same stubbornness."

Gail stopped. "What?"

Femi laughed. "In a good way. Stubborn in a good way."

"It wasn't mine. It was Kay's shadow you saw. It must have been Kay's."

Femi blinked, stiffening at the sharp clean pain in her voice. "No— I... It was yours. I'm sure it was."

Gail fell back against the rain-drenched stone, wet heather prickling her palms. Disappointment leaked out of her like a wound.

"Aren't you going to follow it?" Femi asked. "You have to get it back."

Gail swallowed. "It must have been here. At the Storm Sisters. Why didn't it stay?" She lifted her head to scowl at the two giants leaning over the cliff and noticed Mhirran hurrying towards them. Gail squinted past her for Francis, but he wasn't there.

When Mhirran reached them, she shook her head slightly. "He's heading back." Her voice was small, but lighter somehow, as if all the vowels were breathing out. Her eyes widened expectantly at Gail, who shook her head.

"It was Gail's shadow I saw," Femi explained quietly.

"It was going so fast, but I know it was hers. I've seen it before. When I was drawing the wildcat, it swept right past me. Made me shiver," he added, with a wry smile.

Mhirran's mouth opened and closed. "You saw it when you did the wildcat?"

Femi nodded, eyebrows raised at Mhirran's strange intensity.

"Gail," Mhirran said quickly. "You know that blue whales can talk to each other across thousands of miles in the sea—"

Gail twisted her hair. *Not now, Mhirran. Not now.*

"Well, I thought at first that your shadow was leading us to Kay's, but if Femi says your shadow came past when he was drawing the wildcat early this morning, then it was there first. Do you see? We saw Kay's shadow from there much later. So I think..." Her voice became faster and faster and higher and higher. "I think Kay's shadow has been looking for *your* shadow." Mhirran breathed out and her eyes were sea-bright.

Gail stared. Kay's shadow was looking for hers? No. Mhirran had it wrong.

Then Gail thought back to forever ago when she was sitting at the kitchen table eating cereal. Her own shadow had disappeared just before she took Kay's toast up to her. And then in her bedroom... Maybe she hadn't chased Kay's shadow away after all. She'd been angry and upset and had kicked at it, but maybe Kay's shadow had already made up its mind to follow her own. Had Kay's shadow gone after hers? She shook her head.

"But why?"

Femi added one last stroke of chalk to the turtle and it was complete.

"I know it sounds crazy, wildcat." He grinned. "But maybe she needs you. And if she's looking for your shadow, then we know exactly where she'll be," he said, striding forwards between the rocks towards the path.

Gail stared down at her shadowless feet, which were sore and cold in their muddy shoes. She shook her head. *They've got it so wrong*, she thought. *She doesn't need me. I need her.*

But even as she tried to shake the idea away, the words grew bigger with each step she took. *She needs you, wildcat.*

Gail took a deep breath and turned to follow the others over the lip of the cliff, down the zigzagging path, towards the cove.

Chapter Twenty-four

The path was dented with Femi and Mhirran's hurried footprints as Gail slipped down behind them, kicking sand up into curtains. As she got lower, shells crunched beneath her feet and she peered into small pools, tucked like secrets between seaweed-wigged rocks. She wasn't sure what she was looking for: her own shadow or Kay's?

"Ow." She'd walked straight into Mhirran's back. Mhirran and Femi were frozen, staring towards the sea. Gail followed their gaze. Right at the edge of the water, something dark and huge was stranded on the beach. Gail blinked. It wasn't a shadow.

"What is that?"

"No," Femi said. "No." And his voice was broken.

Gail was running now. Her shoes dug into the sand and the shape grew bigger and bigger. "No no no no no." The word bubbled out of her mouth. "No. No. No."

Hot salty tears flooded her cheeks and the whale

blurred behind them. It lay on its side, the ocean licking its tail like a wound. A sperm whale. Gigantic as the moon. Grey as thunder. Its mouth was open, teeth gleaming within. Gail stopped a metre from it, wiping snot from her nose with a sleeve. The whale's eye was a small planet. Its skin was rippled and wrinkled and webbed with dark grooves. Gail touched the air near its fin.

"I'm sorry. I'm so sorry." Her shoulders shook and she slumped to the sand.

Looking up, she had a clear view of the Storm Sisters standing guard over the cove. She'd just been there. Why hadn't she looked down and seen the whale? She'd been too focused on Francis and his shadow swallower. All her attention had been on the ravine and the river.

But the shadows... The shadows had been at the Storm Sisters. They would not have missed this sea giant, stranded on the beach. They must have followed the cliff path down to it, they must have been here. But now they were nowhere to be seen.

I'm too late, she thought, blinking away tears. *I'm too late.*

At her shoulder, flame-coloured hair tickled her cheek. Mhirran squeezed her hand.

Words shuddered out of Gail. "It's. All. My. Fault."

And she wasn't sure any more whether she meant Kay or the whale.

Mhirran shook her head. "She's beautiful."

Gail pushed the snot and hair around her face and sniffed. "She's broken."

"Couldn't we—"

"No." Gail struggled to breathe. "Out of the water... they're too heavy. Their organs collapse and..."

That's just what Kay had said. Late one night, when Gail was looking for a book in her room. *I feel like my head's too heavy. I can't float any more. I'm like a whale out of water.*

Gail dug her fingernails into her palms. "I left her, Mhirran. I left Kay. I don't mean yesterday. I mean, when she began to sink. Back then, that was when I left her. I let her down."

Mhirran didn't say anything. She didn't say anything in the loudest way Gail had ever heard. It felt like the air shifted and settled again.

"What do I do now?"

"We've got to find your shadows," Mhirran said.

Gail shook her head. "They're not here," she said. "It doesn't matter. It's over."

"It's not over," Mhirran said. Then she squinted out to sea. "Wait..." She gave Gail's hand one last squeeze then walked out towards the tide.

With a quiet cough, Femi squatted beside Gail. "It's a sperm whale isn't it? Someone told me about a pod of sperm whales who took in a dolphin once. They let it swim with them. The dolphin had a bad spine so I guess it couldn't keep up with its own pod. It was unusual, she said. Sperm whales aren't that sociable." Femi chuckled. "She was telling me that because I was so quiet in maths. She wanted more chat. Your sister, I mean."

Sometimes, Gail thought as she thumped the wet sand, *people say exactly the worst thing ever.*

Femi glanced at her blotched face. "At the end of the story, Kay said, 'My sister told me that. My sister told me that about the sperm whales.'" Femi paused.

Gail pushed sand deep beneath her fingernails. Yes, she had. Kay didn't know anything about whales.

"And," Femi continued, "what got me was that was the bit she smiled at – the bit about her sister telling her. She said it like it was the most amazing part of the story."

Gail was quiet. The sea lapped at the whale and salt tanged inside her nostrils. Mhirran was wading now, the water up to her ankles. A seagull cried overhead and clouds raced across the sky, trailing their ragged edges. The rain beat down on their sodden shoulders.

"You were doing the right thing, Gail. You were looking for her shadow."

Gail bit her lip. No one knew about the angry pufferfish deep inside her, or the feel of Kay's shadow as she'd kicked it away. Had she really wanted to find Kay's shadow, or did she just want to run as far away as she could from Kay's sad sinking eyes?

Femi shifted. "Do you still have that pearl?"

Gail nodded, pulling it out of her pocket to give to him.

"You know how I got this?" Femi looked away from Gail, away from the pearl, pressed tight against his palm. "I killed a mussel for it. Cracked open its shell like it was nothing. Fished for it, just like Euan and Gus were going to. It's why they trusted me to know where the mussels were. Because I'd done it before."

Gail swallowed. "No."

"I didn't know..." Femi's voice trailed away. He tugged at his shoelaces and shrugged. "I didn't know it was bad. See, my friend... someone I thought was a friend, told me about it." He shot a sideways glance at Gail. "It's hard for me to make friends, like real friends, when I move somewhere new. Mostly people don't see me. They just see... this." Femi waved his hand across the white spaces in his skin. "So I went with him, and even when I started to think it was wrong, I pretended it wasn't. Until I figured out they were endangered. I didn't know that. And then I stopped. And everything changed."

Gail stared at Femi. "What about your friend?"

"My friend? Nah. He's gone. I mean, he's still here, but we're not friends." Femi took a deep breath. "But it's alright to be wrong, you know, to mess up. Everyone does. As long as you make up for it."

He paused for a moment, then said, "Did I tell you it was Kay's idea to use the ravine? She said I couldn't do it by myself, that she'd help me. She'd pull me back up. She said too many people try to do things by themselves – she couldn't understand it. It's a brave thing to ask for help, she said. The bravest thing." Femi turned to Gail. "And you're not doing this by yourself any more, Gail. You've got us." Femi stretched out and stood up. "So, Kay asked you to get her shadow, right? Let's get it then."

Gail slowly stood up next to him, brushing sand off her knees. "I keep thinking about what Mhirran said about Kay's shadow following mine. Maybe her shadow was chasing after mine because I wasn't there for her. Because I wasn't the person I needed to be. Because I wasn't a gale."

"And your shadow was going to the Storm Sisters?"

Gail frowned. "I thought that's where Kay's was heading. But if her shadow was following mine then it must have been *my* shadow that was going to the Storm Sisters. It's where me and Kay planned to go the next time a storm came. We said we would shelter from the storm together." She paused. "I think my shadow wanted me to follow it here. I think it wanted me to see the Storm Sisters for myself."

Femi turned to look up at the two giants looming over the cliff edge. "Maybe your shadow is trying to tell you something." He pointed. "See the one on the right?" Gail nodded. "That's Eilidh. She's the youngest and the smallest. They say that just as they were being turned to stone, she leaned out across her sister, so that the storms would reach her first. She was trying to protect Mor. Do you see?"

Gail stared at them. Femi was right. The smaller sister edged further over the cliff, her face turned bravely towards the sharp sting of the ocean spray, the grey bulk of her rock bent like a protective arm around her sister.

Gail thought of Kay's hand beneath her stomach when she'd held Gail up in the town pool, and Kay's arm wrapped tight around her as she helped Gail back up the beach when she sliced her ankle. Gail remembered swimming in the sea together for the first time, how they'd tread water laughing, their hands held tight together, and she thought of the cave nestled between the two Storm Sisters, like they shared the same beating heart. Gail swallowed hard. She knew what her shadow was trying to help her understand. "It's my turn now," she whispered. Because the safest place to be in a storm is together.

As Gail turned away, something glimmered for a moment in the corner of her eye.

"Look!" She pointed at Femi's shoe. "It's Leo!"

Femi grinned at the limpet awkwardly. "I told Mhirran I'd take him back. She thinks he came from a beach right by where I live."

Gail bent down and ran a finger along the limpet's wigwam edges. They were rough and welcome against her fingers. It felt like a long time since she'd bumped into Mhirran in the caves. An orange-haired girl chattering in Dolphin and carrying a lost limpet home.

"Gail! Femi! There's another whale!" Mhirran was half-running, half-wading towards them, her face flushed and her legs soaking wet. "It's going to get stuck in shallow water. I think it's looking for this one. We've got to do something. We've got to save it!"

Gail hurried forward, scanning the water. Then she saw it: another whale, dangerously close to the shore. This one was smaller, younger, though still huge, and it seemed to be looking for something. Gail chewed her lip. It was impossible. They couldn't save it. The tide was coming in and the whale was already too close.

Then a strange feeling began at her toes. A warmth

like the end of a journey or her sister's laughter. It flooded her body. Gail looked down. Leo the Limpet's shadow was nestled next to her right boot. Gail blinked. *Limpets can find their own way home.* And as Gail stared at the blue-grey ocean, the waves reaching up the beach in curiosity, the sea felt like the home she'd forgotten she had. It felt like their home: hers and Kay's.

When someone you care about is sinking, Gail's mouth was a determined line through her freckles and she felt the gale rise powerfully inside her, *you never give up trying to save them.*

Chapter Twenty-five

Darts of wind lifted the sea into churning white froth and waves crashed onto the beach, reaching long fingers towards their feet. Gail's hair slapped her cheeks and gusts billowed out her jumper like a man o'war. The swimming whale was closer now. Gail could see the slick wet grey of its back.

I wish Kay was here. The thought was a lump in her throat. Then Gail straightened. She was doing this for Kay. She was Gale and she could do this. She took a deep breath. *Think.* She'd braved Oyster Cave. She'd escaped from the tree-shadow and rescued Mhirran. She'd met a wildcat and trapped the pearl fishers. She'd done all of that without Kay. Rescuing a whale was just like that, right?

"Think, Gail. Think," she whispered. Thunder cracked the sky and water shivered down her back. Gail wiped rain from her eyes and squinted. The whale was even closer. It was trying to reach the one on the shore. Was it her mother? Her sister? Gail winced. How could she turn it around, swim it out to sea again? High above, a bird cried out and Gail saw it spiral upwards towards another. She remembered what Jake had said about the storm petrel shadows. *There are ties between shadows as well, Gail. Stronger ties than we could guess at.* Gail looked back to the stranded whale, which lay like a fallen mountain across the beach. Her eyes stung but she blinked them clear.

"The shadow," she breathed.

"The storm's bringing her closer," Mhirran whispered. "What can we do?"

Gail pushed her hair back. "I have to lead the whale away. I think it's looking for this one." She gestured towards the beached whale. "I'm going to take her shadow."

Mhirran blinked. "No, you can't go in during this storm. Look at the water, Gail. You can't swim in that, it's too dangerous."

Gail looked at Mhirran's earnest, frightened eyes, huge behind her glasses, which were halfway down her nose. Gail pushed them up carefully and smiled. *Of course...* "We need another storm, Mhirran. A storm to fight this one."

Mhirran's eyes widened. "Jake?"

Gail nodded.

"But, how can I...?" Mhirran flapped her hands in the air. "He's afraid of storms. He won't—"

"He will, because you're asking, Mhirran. He cares about you."

Mhirran's face was pale, but she tucked her hair behind her ears. "Okay," she said. "Good luck."

Gail watched Mhirran run back towards the cliff-face and the path. Then she took off her shoes, her rucksack and her jumper. Her teeth were chattering already. Gail stood before the whale on the shore and ran one hand slowly along its rough skin.

"I'm sorry," she whispered. "Will you let me take your shadow? Your friend is in danger."

The shadow was smaller than the whale. It shivered like silk when Gail stepped into it. And when she stepped away, it moved with her like a mountain might move. As if it had all the time in the world.

Gail felt it in her bones and her lungs and the *beat beat* of her heart. She could hear the hum and clicks of the whale's language. She could feel its deep darkness, its intelligence and its yearning for water.

"Thank you," she murmured, and, as she turned towards the ocean, she saw something small and dark stroke the side of the whale's body. The limpet's shadow nestled against the beached whale. It wasn't alone.

As soon as the whale's shadow touched the water, Gail felt lighter. As if she had miles and miles of swimming before her and miles and miles behind. She watched the shadow ripple out along the sea floor.

"This is the first time I've swum alone," she said to nobody in particular.

"No it isn't." Femi replied. He was standing in his top and pants, and the black and white of his skin shone like one of his own beautiful drawings. The water rolled over their feet and rain-veils swung and shifted over the sea.

When she twisted round, Gail could see a small figure on top of the cliff. She looked tiny. Her hands were cupped around her mouth but Gail couldn't hear her. A burst of birds punctured the sky further away and Gail realised that Mhirran was calling them. She was calling the birds so Jake would see them, and know she needed him. She looked like a lighthouse, Gail thought, as Mhirran's hair shone orange against the grey sky. Gail remembered Lighthouse Rock. *Because you light up the ocean...*

She frowned at the waves. Was the water too rough? Was it too dangerous? Then one of the birds she'd seen circling high above plummeted downwards, sweeping past her cheek, letting out a familiar *Krrrrrrhuh Krrrrrrrhuh.* Stunned, Gail turned to spot a thin, dark figure watching them from the edge of the beach. As she stared, the figure gave a slow nod, gesturing slightly at the bird shadows and the ocean. It was a small gesture, but Gail knew exactly what he meant.

"Who's that?" Femi asked.

"It's Francis," breathed Gail. "He's saying the bird shadows will look out for us."

"Francis? But didn't he...?"

"People make mistakes," she said, smiling at Femi. Then she closed her eyes and squeezed his hand, filling her face with determination.

He grinned. "All right," he said, and they walked into the ocean together as the skies thundered above them and rain splashed onto their cheeks.

Chapter Twenty-six

Cold, Gail thought as her teeth clattered together, *is too short a word for such a horrible thing.* Four letters weren't enough for the bone-crushing, needle-stinging, eye-aching, tongue-numbing cold of the ocean. It bit the air from her lungs and the muscle from her arms. Swimming felt impossible. Even the whale's shadow couldn't keep her warm.

"I-i-f y-you k-k-k-eep m-m-moving you'll w-warm u-u-up." Femi thrashed hopefully in the water next to her.

Gail tried to say something back to him but her lips wouldn't move. All she was thinking was: *OW. Owowowowow. Ow.* The bird shadows were swooping low over them, like strange feathery lifeguards.

When Gail kicked her feet, she felt something loosen beneath her.

"F-F-emi, I-I'm... T-the shadow... It's t-t-t-t-t-oo d-d-d-de-e-ep-p."

She swallowed, lifted up both her feet and looked down. The shadow was still there, large and looming and fragile on the bottom. Seaweed stroked its darkness. *Okay*, Gail thought, *it's not going to leave me.*

They pushed against the current and held their breath when waves crashed over their heads. Gail's arms ached from breaststroke, and her feet kicked weakly at the water. The whale was getting nearer, but, when Gail looked back, the shore wasn't getting further away. Panic rose in her throat. She tried to swim faster but waves pummelled against them, pushing them back towards the beach. She closed her eyes and willed herself forward.

"Ga—"

Gail didn't see the wave in time. Saltwater rushed up her nose and into her mouth. She gagged and thrashed at the water and when she broke the surface, one bird shadow was pulling at her arm and seaweed hung from her hair.

"The current's t-too strong." Femi was gasping for breath. "We'll n-never m-make it."

Gail ignored him. She had to reach the whale. Blood drummed inside her head and her arms felt like rocks. *Think of the sunfish*, she thought. *It's so heavy but it still floats.* The rain was falling in a thick sheet from the sky, biting into their eyes and face like hail. Gail strained and kicked against the pull of the ocean. But it wasn't working. And the whale was closer than ever to the shore.

Then she felt something push her forward, like a hand on her back. Then again. A strong wind was helping her out to sea, leaning against her shoulders and whispering in her hair. Gail blinked. The water was changing. The waves were hesitating, rising to a peak and then falling back on themselves, confused. Rain was driven horizontal and, for a startling moment, lifted upwards. The sea was shifting, shivering, then, achingly slowly, tugging Gail and Femi and the whale away from the shore.

Jake had arrived.

Now Gail and Femi were level with the whale, away to its left. It was still facing towards the shore, towards its stranded friend. "I have to lead it away," she shouted over the wind. "You go between it and the beach. Don't get too close."

Half of her words were swallowed by the gale, but Femi shook his head. "I'm staying with you."

"Trust me," she shouted. Then, because it sounded good and made her fingers ache a bit less, she shouted it again. "Trust me!"

After she shouted it the third time and spat out a mouthful of seawater, Femi had disappeared, one of the petrel shadows hovering by his head. *Okay*, Gail thought. *Just a bit further.*

By the time she'd swum around so that she was out beyond the whale, Gail had decided that she would never ever swim again. She hurt all over and she was sure something was biting her. And her plan wasn't working. Despite Femi thrashing in front of it, and Gail and the shadow trying to draw it away, the whale was still headed for shallow water.

But then the massive creature began to turn.

It happened slowly, like the sun rising. The water shifted around its body as its tail moved through the ocean. Further beyond it, Gail could see the spray lifting where Femi was splashing and swimming up and down between the whale and the beach.

She looked down. The water was far too deep for her toes to reach the seabed and too dark for her to see the shadow. But she felt it. It was stretching, reaching out towards the turning whale and then retreating back to Gail, guiding it towards her. Gail began to tread water, rain drumming on her head and shoulders and the wind stinging her cheeks.

"This way," she said, the words rippling towards the whale. "This way, where the water's deeper."

She floated on her back, kicking her feet and swilling her arms backwards, feeling the shadow beneath her gently steer the whale away from the shore. Behind Gail, the stranded whale was a smudge on the beach, a smudge like a tearstain in ink.

"I'm sorry," Gail murmured. "But it's this way."

The whale was so close now, Gail could feel the ocean parting before it. For the first time, she thought about how huge it was and how small she was in comparison. Fear gripped her throat and she struggled to stay afloat. And then the whale passed her, and the shadow at her feet went with it. It moved so close she could feel the tickle of its fin. It was only an arm's length away when a volcano of air erupted out of its blowhole. Gail tipped her face up to it: a whale's breath. And, in that instant, watching the whale swim towards the horizon, Gail coughed around a mouthful of seawater and saw something small and spiky swim out from inside her into the vastness of the sea. The pufferfish had gone.

Gail watched the whale until she could no longer see it. She wasn't angry any more and she didn't feel helpless. She felt light and glowing. She felt fierce and free. She felt tired and cold and wet. And a long way from the beach.

When she turned towards the shore, the wind hit her face like a wet flannel. Gail reeled back, then was knocked forward by a wave and spiralled round until she was facing out to sea again. Where was Jake?

The second time, she got further. But her legs were numb now and dragged behind her. The whale's shadow had gone. Gail was alone.

She pushed her fringe from her eyes but the waves grew like hills and the beach disappeared from view. She felt so tired. So so tired. Her hands grasped at the water. She needed something to hold on to.

And as another wave churned her over, her nan's words flooded her mind. *The sea en' got no back door, Gail. Remember that when you're swimming. Remember that you can hold your breath longer than Kay.* Gail took a deep breath and dived underwater, where the waves couldn't choke her. She beat against the current. And when she surfaced she was close enough to see them: Mhirran dancing on the sand, saying something in a strange code that Gail didn't understand; Jake, collapsed exhausted next to her; Francis, tall and still at the edge of the beach; and Femi, his head dipping in and out of the water steadily as he front-crawled towards her.

The smile started at her feet, warming each toe before flowing around her knees and into her stomach and her ribcage and her shoulders and her ears and her eyes. It felt bigger than a whale, bigger than a mountain, bigger than the sea. Gail grinned and her feet kicked and her arms pushed against the water as Femi drew level with her and they swam the last stretch to the shore together.

When, at last, Gail crawled onto the beach, blue-lipped and bedraggled, the smile glittered in her eyes like a thousand luminous jellyfish. And when she stood, with seaweed curled around her ankles, two shadows stretched and rippled from her feet.

Gail was a wildcat, a lighthouse, a gale. And she had found their shadows.

Chapter Twenty-seven

A watery sun slipped through the curtains onto the pillow. Gail watched the light play over Kay's eyelids and twist around the green seaweed strands in her hair. Her breathing was like the sea's whisper on a beach. It was early. Gail was the only one awake. And Femi, of course, but he was outside.

When they'd got back last night, after Mhirran's uncle had found them at the cove, Kay was already asleep. Gail's mum had shouted and cried and grounded Gail for three hundred years and then given her a bone-crushing hug and made them all macaroni pie. After dinner, once they'd taught everyone how to say 'wildcat' in Morse code, Mhirran and her uncle had headed home to Francis. He had wandered north soon after Gail and Femi crawled onto the beach, and Jake had followed after him, his eyes shadowed and soft.

Gail and Femi had made the plan for early this morning before Femi had left her house. It was Gail who'd found the paint.

Kay stirred in her sleep, her shadow rippling with the movement, and Gail froze. Now that she was back, Gail didn't know what to say. There was too much to say. Kay twitched and a strand of hair fell across her cheek. Gail tucked it neatly behind her ear. The freckles on her sister's cheek were like stars. What would Mhirran say? Gail grinned and took a deep breath.

"Did you know that whales can speak across thousands of miles and that storms have pockets and the sea is colder without you?"

Kay opened her eyes and blinked.

"Hi," Gail said.

"Hi."

Kay's eyes were just as she remembered them. Sad and so far away. Gail swallowed. "I'm sor—"

"You found it." A sudden smile tugged at Kay's mouth. She pointed at the carpet. "You found it," she said again and there was the shine of scales in her voice.

Gail's eyes widened. Kay wasn't pointing at her own shadow at all. She was pointing to Gail's. Mhirran was right. Kay's shadow had been trying to find Gail's all along. Gail bit her lip and rubbed at her nose. Something wobbled inside her eyes. "We got yours back too. And there's something I want to show you." Gail gestured to the window. "I asked my friend to make it for you."

Kay raised her eyes at 'friend' and slowly, carefully, pulled herself out of the bed. Gail took her hand. "Because when you're sinking," she said, "you always need something to hold on to."

She opened the curtain. On the grey side wall of the newsagent next door, Femi had painted their story. He'd painted a huge sunfish, round and glowing, the water around it filled with swirls and jellyfish. He'd painted a limpet, small and determined, and two shadowy storm petrels spinning through the air. He'd painted a mimic octopus pretending to be a sea snake and a leafy seadragon disappearing amongst a ripple of seaweed. He'd painted the two Storm Sisters, sharing one cave-heart between them, Eilidh leaning protectively across Mor. He'd painted a young sperm whale, swimming away towards the horizon, in a blue-grey sea. And, in the middle of the wall, he'd painted a manta ray leaping high over a wildcat, whilst all around them were the quick swirls and eddies of a strong wind, like the wind of change or adventure – like the wind of a gale.

Kay gasped and there, deep deep in her eyes, Gail saw a light gleaming, like the glow from a far-off ship, or a star. As they stood, hand in hand staring at their world, Gail's shadow stretched dark and silk-grey next to Kay's, saying

I am here

I am here

I am here.

Acknowledgements

As a child, I used to begin notebooks by writing: *This is the story that I will finish.* Of course, I never did finish them, so it is with some astonishment and much pride that I find myself at the end of this story. My ten-year-old self would be delighted, and I owe thanks to a great many people for helping me along the way.

Firstly, thank you to my beta readers. Thank you to my younger sister, Martha Ilett, for reading multiple drafts with enthusiasm, and to Caitlyn McHarge, Claire Martin and Quinn Ramsay. Your questions, insight and encouragement were utterly invaluable in propelling me onwards through the early drafts. Thank you also to Carly Brown for the much-needed cake-and-writing chats, and to Ashanti Harris and Nicole Culp for your generous feedback.

Thank you to my editors, Eleanor Collins and Jennie Skinner, the most committed and considerate editors I could hope for. I've learned so much from you and you have brought clarity to a sprawling, strange story. Thank you to Leah and the design team for this stunning cover and thank you to everyone at Floris Books; I feel extremely lucky to be supported by such an incredible team.

For their encouragement when I was just beginning to write children's fiction, I would like to thank my creative writing tutors, Dr Carolyn Jess-Cooke and Dr Eleanor Rees. Thank you to Mairi Hedderwick and Moniack Mhor for the opportunity to meet wonderful writers in a beautiful place, and to Wigtown Book Festival for trusting in me; it was an honour to be Children's Writer in Residence in 2015.

The research for this book took me to many places, but I'd particularly like to acknowledge contributors to *National Geographic*, who are responsible for my deep enthusiasm for wobbegongs, leafy seadragons, pinecone fish and many more wonderful and intriguing creatures. What a world there is in the ocean to learn about, and to protect against our misdoings.

Thank you to everyone who asked me how the writing was going; your questions pushed this procrastinator forward. Thank you to Jessy for the laughter, the adventures, and for holding my hand through the tricky bits; thank you to Moa, for your writing and friendship; thank you to Nicole and Farah for your beautiful encouragement; and to Sogol, Ashanti, Romany and Julia: you inspire, challenge and support me in the best way. Thank you to everyone at Glasgow Women's Library, I feel so lucky to be surrounded by so many incredible women.

Finally, thank you to my mum and dad for nurturing within me a love of words and stories from such a young age. Thank you to my sisters, Hannah and Martha, for always being there for me. And to all my family, I'm so grateful for your support and excitement for my writing.

And thank you, reader, for swimming alongside Gail.

About the Author

Emily Ilett studied at the Glasgow School of Art and the University of Glasgow. She was awarded the Mairi Hedderwick Writing for Children Bursary from Moniack Mhor in 2015, and was Children's Writer in Residence at Wigtown Book Festival the same year. *The Girl Who Lost Her Shadow*, her first novel, won the Kelpies Prize for new Scottish children's writing in 2017.

You may also enjoy...

'Perfect for fans of magic and Harry Potter.' – Sharleen Creasey, Seven Stories Bookshop

'The Nowhere Emporium is up there with Ollivanders as a magical place that readers will want to explore again and again.' – The Guardian

Winner of the Blue Peter Best Story Award 2016 and the Scottish Children's Book Awards 2016.

When Daniel stumbles into the mysterious Nowhere Emporium in Glasgow, he opens the door to a world of breathtaking magic and looming danger.

 Also available as an eBook

DiscoverKelpies.co.uk

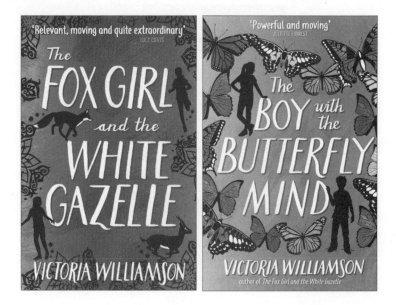

Discover two beautifully-written and powerful novels from critically-acclaimed children's author Victoria Williamson.

In *The Fox Girl and the White Gazelle*, a refugee and a bully – Reema and Caylin – can't imagine being friends, until a shared secret brings them together.

The Boy with the Butterfly Mind is an uplifting and positive depiction of a young boy with ADHD. As Jamie's chaotic life collides with ordered Elin, sparks fly. But they soon realise that, just like families, happy ever afters come in all shapes and sizes.

 Also available as an eBook

DiscoverKelpies.co.uk

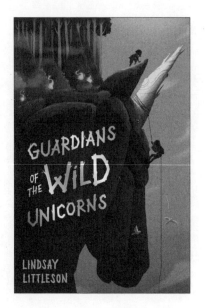

'An adventure tale that melds the real and the fantastic with warmth and humour.' – The Herald

'Mixes mythology and suspense in a contemporary page turner.' – Book Trust

In the wild Scottish highlands, best friends Lewis and Rhona discover that the legends are true: unicorns are real creatures, darkly magical and in deadly danger. Can the friends rescue the wild unicorns before an ancient promise has unimagined consequences for them all?

 Also available as an eBook

DiscoverKelpies.co.uk